"Y... ...od head for business."

Claire knew exactly where h... ...s going with this and chose not to f... ...y. Well. Give everyone m... ...l... ... ...say "—best. And h...

"You, to... ...hers. And she thoug...

Because, ...pped out to her car, the thought nagged that despite what she'd wanted to see—to believe—about things easing between them…had they really? If they'd truly settled into friendship—which was the only logical choice, given the circumstances—why had that conversation felt like a pair of shoes that didn't fit?

"Don't even bother answering that," she muttered to the universe.

Which was probably laughing its damn ass off.

***

Jersey Boys:
Born…raised…and ready.

SANTA'S PLAYBOOK

BY
KAREN TEMPLETON

Published in Great Britain 2014
by Mills & Boon, an imprint of Harlequin (UK) Limited,
Eton House, 18-24 Paradise Road, Richmond, Surrey, TW9 1SR

© 2014 Karen Templeton-Berger

ISBN: 978-0-263-91334-7

23-1114

Harlequin (UK) Limited's policy is to use papers that are natural, renewable and recyclable products and made from wood grown in sustainable forests. The logging and manufacturing processes conform to the legal environmental regulations of the country of origin.

Printed and bound in Spain
by CPI, Barcelona

A recent inductee into the Romance Writers of America Hall of Fame, three-time RITA® Award-winning author **Karen Templeton** has written more than thirty novels for Mills & Boon. She lives in New Mexico with two hideously spoiled cats, has raised five sons and lived to tell the tale, and could not live without dark chocolate, mascara and Netflix.

To the people in my life
Both those I've known
And those I've yet to meet
Who've made Christmas magic for me.
I love you all.

Chapter One

Today would have been his sixteenth anniversary.

Only half hearing the kids' thudding and slamming and yelling from downstairs, Ethan Noble glanced out his bedroom window, where a pair of chattering squirrels chased each other through an oak tree, the bare branches thickly webbed against a pale November sky. It'd been cold and windy that day, too, the mottled clouds occasionally spitting on everybody's windshields as they made their way to All Saints.

But nobody'd cared. About the weather, about the indisputable fact that Merri's stomach bulged a little underneath her high-waisted wedding dress. So things'd happened slightly out of order. Since it'd all worked out like they'd always planned anyway, what difference did it make—?

His cell buzzed—an incoming text message. Only one

person who'd call this early. And for only one reason.
Ethan scooped the phone off his nightstand.

Thinking of you.

If anyone would understand what he was feeling today
it'd be the man who'd adopted Ethan when he was a tod-
dler. Also a widower for some years now, Preston Noble
had set an example of strength and loyalty and fairness
that Ethan could only hope to emulate, especially as a parent. And his father had adored Merri....

God, she'd been beautiful. And so fricking happy.
Same as he'd been, even if Juliette's precipitous appearance hadn't been in the playbook. Merri, though... She'd
been a part of his playbook since they were fifteen.

Juliette's age, he thought as his daughter appeared in the
doorway, her wavy, warm brown hair streaked with some
god-awful color. At least it was only chalk, it washed out,
but still. Lime-green?

"Um...the others had breakfast, sorta. Cereal, anyway.
So...I'm ready to go—?"

"Sure," Ethan said, smiling. "We're good."

Jules came over, standing on tiptoe to give him a hug, a
peck on his scratchy cheek. Shaving was strictly optional
on the weekends. Then she released him, eyes full of concern, and Ethan's stung. He didn't make an issue of the anniversary, so the younger kids were oblivious. But Jules...
She knew. In fact, she already had her eye on Merri's wedding dress, packed up safe in the special heirloom box in
Ethan's closet. Never mind she was already three inches
taller than her mother.

"You know, I don't have to go—"

"It's only another Saturday, honey. So get outta here,"
he said in an exaggerated Jersey accent. "Do your mom
proud, okay?"

"Okay," she said, and started off, only to spin around at the door. "I'll do a real breakfast when I get back. How's that?"

"Whatever," Ethan said, loving her so much it hurt. And not only because she was the spitting image of Merri, except for her eyes, more green-blue than purple-blue. But because he'd look at her and think, *How'd I luck out to get one this good?*

Unlike the twins, he thought on a brief chuckle as the boys bellowed downstairs. Then Isabella had arrived, a surprise after a six-year dry spell, to more than outshine her brothers in the Tasmanian devil department—

Briefly, resentment stabbed that his youngest daughter would never know her mother.

But like always, he shrugged off the memories, the self-pity and anger and—even after all this time—the disbelief as he slowly descended the stairs, his palm lightly raking the dark wood banister's numerous dings and gouges that long preceded his and Merri's buying the house four blocks from the high school, right after the twins were born. At the bottom he flexed his knee, willing the ache to subside: coaching peewee football was a lot more physical than high school varsity.

He'd no sooner reached the kitchen than the three remaining kids accosted him about a dozen things needing his immediate attention—hell, even the dog whined to go outside. But Ethan found the bombardment comforting, even reassuring, in its life-as-usual normalcy. So, as he let out the dog and returned the kids' verbal volleys and poured more milk for Bella and double-checked the schedule on the fridge so they wouldn't be late for the twins' game, he gave silent thanks for the day-to-day craziness that kept him sane.

That kept him focused, not on what he'd lost, but on what he still had.

Even when his gaze caught, prominently displayed on the family room wall twenty feet beyond the kitchen, the wedding portrait of those two crazy-in-love twenty-two-year-olds, grinning like they had all the time in the world to figure life out.

Happy anniversary, babe, he silently wished the only woman he'd ever loved.

Ancient floorboards creaked underfoot in the over-heated Queen Anne as Claire Jacobs methodically assessed the leavings from someone's life. She yanked off her heavy knit hat, shaking her curls free. *Poodle hair,* her mother had called it. Smiling, Claire lifted a lovely cut-glass bowl to check the price. Only to nearly drop it. This was an estate sale, for cripes' sake. Not Sotheby's.

As if reading her mind, some prissy old dude in a tweed jacket squinted at her from several feet away. Ignoring him, Claire replaced the bowl and glanced around at the jumble of furniture and accessories and tchotchkes, all moping like rejected props from *Mad Men.* And for this she'd dragged her butt out of bed on one of the few mornings she could actually sleep in—?

Wait… She scurried across the room to practically snatch the leaded-glass lamp off the table. Okay, it was hardly Tiffany, not for twenty bucks, but it would look terrific on that little table by her front door—

"Miss Jacobs?"

Clutching her prize, Claire twisted around…and grinned. "Juliette! What are you doing here?"

Sporting a denim jacket, a blinged-out hoodie and preppy shorts worn over patterned tights, Claire's student flashed a mouthful of metal punctuated by hot pink ties. "We live a few houses down," she said, and Claire's stomach pinched. Since "we" included Hoover High's ridiculously good-looking, widowed football coach, the object of probably most of Maple River's postpubescent female fantasies. Except Claire, of course, who was above such folderol. Stomach pinching aside. "So I figured I'd check it out," the teen said, "see what was good."

"Not sure there's much that would appeal to a teenager," Claire said even as Juliette zeroed in on a demitasse collection, carefully picking up one of the cups and holding it to the light.

"Oh, I'm not looking for myself." She scrutinized another cup. "It's for my business."

"Your…business?"

"Used to be my mom's. She'd buy stuff at estate sales and flea markets, then sell it on eBay. She was pretty good at it, too." This said matter-of-factly as the girl sidled over to a stash of old books. "She taught me what to look for, how to price things and stuff. So a few months ago I decided to try selling some pieces myself."

"And is it working?"

"It is." Juliette selected a couple of the books, tucking them to her side. "Which is great, since it'll help pay for college. Depending on where I go, of course." Another sparkling grin accompanied her words. "I'd have to sell a boatload of stuff to afford Yale."

Claire's heart twisted. Although she'd only been teaching a few months—a fork in her life path she could have never predicted—she knew it was wrong to have favorites. And truthfully she loved all "her" kids. Not only her drama students, but even the less-than-motivated ones in her English classes who groaned every time she made them dredge correctly spelled words from their iPodded/Padded/ Phoned brains and *write them down*. By hand. On paper.

But this one was special, for many reasons, not the least of which was her plucky, wide-eyed determination to not only succeed at something at which few did, but also her refusal to feel sorry for herself. Or let anyone else feel sorry for her either, despite losing her mother so young. A stroke, she'd heard. At thirty-five. No prior symptoms, no warning… How scary must that have been? For all of them. Claire had been a little younger than Juliette when her dad died—suddenly, like Juliette's mom—and she'd been stunned by how tenaciously the pain had clung. And yet, if Juliette was suffering from bitterness or resentment, Claire sure as hell couldn't see it.

"There are plenty of drama programs besides Yale's, you know," she said as Juliette carted two of the delicate cups and saucers to the table. "And it would definitely be cheaper to go to school in-state." Claire's sole option, when her mother had barely made enough to keep them housed and fed, let alone fund her only child's college education.

"Yeah, I know." Juliette meticulously stacked books, a few old toys, other odds and ends that Claire wouldn't have thought worth squat next to the cups. Mr. Tweed frowned, but Juliette seemed unfazed, returning to poke through the offerings on another table. "But not a lot of schools that people will actually take your theater degree *seriously*."

Except—as Claire knew only too well—when you're one of a gazillion actresses auditioning for the same part, the invisible director sitting in the dark theater doesn't give a damn where you got your degree. Or even if you have one. However, she was hardly going to burst a fifteen-year-old's bubble.

Juliette carted over a few more cups. "And, yeah, I know I'll have to keep my grades up like crazy, and that's not even *counting* the audition. But it's dumb to admit defeat before you've even tried, right? At least that's what Mom always said."

Claire paid for her lamp, which seemed to slightly mollify old Tweedledee. "Very true. And…your dad? Is he on board with your plans?"

"Sure," Juliette said quickly, poking her hair behind an

ear only slightly less studded than Claire's. "And anyway, I've got a couple years to figure it out, so…" She stopped, frowning at her growing collection. Tweedy glowered.

"Problem, young lady?"

"Yeah. My eyes are bigger than my arms. Um…if I pay for everything now, would you mind if I take it in several trips? Since I walked over here—"

"I could give you a lift," Claire said.

Big blue eyes met hers. "You sure?"

"Absolutely."

"Okay, then. Thanks!" Juliette dug her wallet out of the worn Peruvian-style shoulder bag she always carried as the guy added up her purchases. "Guess this is what you'd call…serendipity. See—I remembered from that vocab list last week. I am so gonna rock my SATs." Then she sighed. "The language part, anyway. Because I totally suck at math. Like Mom did. It's like a genetic curse."

Claire smiled. "What about your father?"

Rolling her eyes, the girl handed over a wad of cash to Tweedsie as a woman wearing a matching scowl wrapped the breakables in tissue paper, placing them in a cardboard box that had once housed cans of little Friskies. "He did his best when I was in middle school, and I didn't flunk, so that's something. But there's a reason he teaches PE."

And clearly the girl had also inherited her mother's sense of humor, since from what little interaction Claire'd had with Juliet's father, she doubted he had one. "Then, maybe you should start working with a tutor. Get a leg up before it gets any harder."

"Omigod—it gets *harder?*"

This said with a twinkle in those blue-green eyes, a flash of dimples. Shaking her head at the teen's giggle, Claire hauled a bag of unbreakables off the table and started toward the front door, holding the lamp aloft like Lady Liberty's torch. Juliette followed with the first of three boxes, which they loaded into the trunk of the ten-year-old Ford Taurus that had belonged to Claire's mother. A few minutes later they pulled up in front of a dignified but slightly weathered twenties-era Tudor...and Claire fell immediately in love.

Not that she felt inclined to two-time her adorable apartment, wedged under the eaves of an even older Queen Anne on the other side of town. It was quirky and funky and all sorts of other -y words, and she adored it. But this house, with its dark wood trim and gabled roof and ivy scrambling up one corner to tickle one of the windows... Wow. Of course, three weeks before Thanksgiving the forty-foot oak on one side was bare, but a pair of frosted spruces glistened in the sun, and a little curl of fireplace smoke teased the bright blue sky, hinting at the warmth inside.

And this charming house was where Ethan Noble lived. Huh.

Claire popped the trunk and got out, figuring she'd help Juliette haul her loot inside, then scram. Except before they got through the slightly scratched up front door, adorned with a slightly sorry fall wreath, not only did the cutest, fuzziest, little white dog trot over to say hi, but Juliette said, "Hey—have you had breakfast? I make awesome omelets. And I'm sure Dad put coffee on, there's always coffee when he's home. Or I could make hot chocolate?"

Yes, Claire could smell the coffee, singing to her like it was auditioning for *The Voice*. But again, getting overly chummy with a student... Not a good idea under the best of circumstances. Getting chummy with one whose father practically gave Claire the evil eye whenever they ran into each other...

"That's lovely of you to offer, but—"

"Pleeease?" Juliette said, and the coffee crooned a little more sweetly, and Claire's stomach growled, and she thought, *Oh, what the hell?*

"You really make good omelets?" she said, and the girl squealed and clapped her hands, yeesh, and the dog did a little dance on its hind legs, and then an absolutely adorable little squirt wearing half her closet barreled down the stairs and right into Juliet's thighs, prattling on about *stupid* Harry and *dumb* Finn and how much she hated, hated, *hated* boys, and Claire got a little dizzy.

Juliette, however, calmly set her box on a nearby table and crouched in front of her baby sister, brushing back a tangle of pale blond hair from a very pissed-looking little face. "So what'd they do this time?" she asked, and the child rattled off a litany of offenses, which were then interrupted by a very masculine but somewhat weary "Bella. Enough."

Followed by a silence thick enough to slice.

"Hey, Dad," Juliette said, standing, then twisting her baby sister around in front of her like a shield. "Look who I ran into at the estate sale! And she gave me a ride home. So I invited her to breakfast. I didn't think you'd mind."

Oh, dear. Was that adolescent defiance rearing its pretty little head? Only, before Claire could process that little tidbit, a certain steely blue gaze rammed into hers—speaking of pissed—and a thousand ancient insecurities tried to rear *their* heads, and she thought *no.*

Or, more exactly, *Hell,* no.

Hey, she'd survived an ever-changing cast of roommates in more New York apartments than she cared to count, not to mention pointless cattle call auditions and insane directors and leering weirdos on the subway, capped off by caring for her dying mother back here in Maple River for nearly a year. A weenie, she was not. Not now, anyway. So no way was a pair of hot blue eyes slinging her back to that hellacious era when she hated her hair/body/

clothes and a cute boy's smile would render her a blithering, klutzy idiot.

Not that she'd actually ever seen Ethan smile. Although he was cute. In a brooding, Brontë-dude sort of way. Even if she hadn't known he was ex-military, his posture and close-cropped hair—a dirty blond, maybe?—would have given him away. He was maybe a hair over six feet tall, but his bearing was…fierce. She imagined he was hell in football practice. Even though she'd never heard any of his players bad-mouth him. Ever.

"Your home is…" Claire glanced around, taking in the clutter of toys and sports equipment smothering what had probably at one time been nice furniture in mostly tans and reds and dark greens…the charred-brick fireplace… the mantel choked with family photos. From some unidentifiable part of the house, an obviously ticked-off male child bellowed, immediately followed by an even louder bellow in response. Claire turned back, smiling. "Lovely. Thank you for having me."

"You're welcome," Ethan mumbled, then yelled up the stairs. "Guys! Come pick up your crap! We've got company!"

"Aw, Dad…"

"Jeez, Dad!" Juliette chirped.

Ethan stabbed a dark look in her direction before turning again, shouting, *"Now!"*

Sneakered feet thundered down the wooden treads, attached to a pair of gangly, shaggy-haired tweens—one blond, one red-haired—who threw Claire a mildly curious glance before attacking the mess. And she had to admit she felt a pang of sympathy for Ethan, raising four kids by himself. There had only been one of her, and both of her parents, and as a kid she'd been way too much of a scaredy-pants to rock the boat. But this—the boys vroomed around the room like a multilimbed dust devil, snatching up equipment and tossing it more *at* than *in* what Claire assumed was a mudroom off the kitchen—was Crazyville. *You hear that, ovaries—?*

Ah. The glare was once more aimed in her direction. Over, she realized, Bella's head, who'd somewhere along the way ended up in her daddy's arms. Strong, muscled arms underneath a gray fleece pullover that emphasized the equally muscled, broad shoulders carrying the weight, if not of the entire world, at least the world that was his.

Realizing Juliette had disappeared—to the kitchen, Claire presumed—she said in a low voice, "I don't mean to intrude—"

"It's okay," he muttered through a jaw that redefined *tight.* "Jules likes to cook, but it's mostly lost on her brothers and sister." His eyes dropped to the little girl clinging to him like a baby monkey, his expression softening. Sort of. "Can't get this one to eat eggs for anything."

"Because eggs are *gross,*" Bella said, making a face exactly like her father's, and it was everything Claire could do not to laugh. Then the little one leaned back, frowning into her father's eyes. "And could you *please* tell Harry an' Finn to stop calling me a *baby*. It hurts my feelings."

Ethan frowned back. "Then you have to promise to stay out of their room. You know it bugs them when you go in there."

"But I want to see Spot!"

"You can see Spot when he's out in his ball."

"But they never take him out anymore!"

"Okay. I'll talk to them, see if we can arrange visitation. Deal?"

After a second, the little girl pushed out a long sigh. "Deal."

"Good." Ethan set her down, cupping her head for a moment before she took off to another part of the house, sparkly sneakers flashing as she ran. He watched her for a moment, then turned back to Claire, muttering, "I'll take eighty hormone-crazed teenage boys over one six-year-old girl, any day."

Wait. Were her ears deceiving her, or was that Ethan Noble making a funny? Well, hell.

"So who's Spot?" she asked when she found her voice again.

"A hamster. The boys named him. So...you ran into Jules?"

"At that estate sale, yeah. I bought a lamp. She bought... a lot more."

One side of his mouth lifted. More chagrin than grin, though. "Sounds about right."

"She's really good at the eBay thing?"

"She really is." He paused, the faint glow in his blue eyes dimming. "Exactly like her mother. I gave Jules fifty bucks seed money. I've lost count of how many times she's multiplied it since them. Kid has a real head for business." Pride glowed through his words, if not on his face, and Claire felt a slight...ping. Of what, she wasn't sure.

"Then she has choices about what to do with her life," Claire said, and Ethan's brow furrowed. "If she's serious about an acting career—"

"Not happening," he said, effectively ending the discussion. But although something in Claire prickled at the dismissal, this was not her battle to fight. Especially since Juliette could easily change her mind a dozen times between now and graduation.

So she smiled and changed the subject. "Mmm... breakfast smells great, doesn't it—?"

"Just so you know," Ethan said, his eyes locked on her face, "my daughter's on a mission."

Now Claire frowned. "What kind of mission?"

"To get herself a stepmother."

An idea with which, judging from his expression, Ethan was not even remotely on board.

Which was fine with Claire, since that was one role she wasn't even inclined to audition for.

Ethan's brows dipped when Claire clamped a hand over her mouth to, apparently, stifle a laugh.

"And you seriously think," she whispered after she lowered her hand, "that's why she invited me to breakfast?"

"Odds are," Ethan said, not sharing Claire's merriment. "You'd be the—let's see—third woman in the past six months she's tried to throw in my path."

This time, a piece of that laugh broke loose to float in his direction, and Ethan felt his shoulders tense. That laugh… It'd been his introduction to the woman before he'd even seen her, during prep week back in late August. A sound far too low and gutsy to come out of someone so small, he remembered thinking when they'd finally met, and her smile had arrowed into him hard enough to make him flinch, her handshake as firm as any man's. Now he literally stepped aside in a lame attempt to dodge that laugh. Not to mention the grin. Although there wasn't a damn thing he could do to avoid the deep brown eyes. Except look away, he supposed. But that would be rude.

"I'm sorry, I know it's not funny for you," she said, but not as if she really meant it. Then she shook her head, making all those curls quiver.

Those curls drove him nuts. Shiny. Soft. Bouncy—

No.

She grinned. "And here I thought we were bonding over a mutual love of the theater."

Ethan bristled. Yeah. That. Or rather, that, *too.* Then again, knowing Jules, the stagestruck phase would in all likelihood go the way of the photography phase and the piano phase and a dozen other phases he didn't even half remember anymore. This matchmaking thing, though, was something else again. He resisted the temptation to massage his knee, acting up despite his telling it not to. He loved Jersey, Jersey was home, but the damp weather sucked.

"Afraid not."

Something like sympathy shone in her eyes, and he bristled again. After three years, you'd think the pity wouldn't bother him anymore. "Then why'd you invite me to stay for breakfast?"

"I didn't. Jules did."

"But..."

"I didn't want to come across like some hard-ass, okay?"

Her mouth curved. No lipstick. Or any other makeup that Ethan could tell. Not that she needed it, with her dark brows and lashes—

Yeah, it bugged him, bugged him like hell, this dumb physical attraction to the woman. Because he had no business being attracted to anybody right now, especially some cute little bouncy-haired drama teacher who was obviously feeding his way-too-impressionable daughter a load of bull. Man, Juliette's constant yammering about the woman was about to drive him up the wall. Even though he knew this was only a crush—although considering how many of the teachers at Hoover were barely younger than the school's namesake, he could hardly blame her.

Any more than he could blame himself, he supposed, for the not-so-little pings and dings and buzzings when Claire was around. He thought he'd buried his libido with his wife. Clearly not.

And this despite her dressing crazier than the kids. Take today, for instance—a sweater that came practically to her knees, the ugliest, puffiest vest on God's green earth, boots that looked like Chewbacca's feet. Three pairs of earrings. Granted, all tiny, but...

"Honestly, I had no idea the kid had an ulterior motive," Claire was saying. "Nor would I have gone along with her nefarious plan if I had—" Something crashed overhead, shaking the house. She looked up. "Because that would drive me nuts."

"You don't like kids?"

Her gaze snapped to his, and Ethan's face heated. A knee-jerk reaction, totally uncalled for and way out of proportion to the situation. Especially considering how often his progeny drove him nuts, too.

Claire tilted her head, a little grin tugging at her mouth. "Kids are great. Noise, not so much. Which is why I love teaching—I can get my fill of the little darlings, then they go home. To someone else's house. And I go home to mine." Harry yelled at Finn about...something. "Where it's, you know, peaceful."

Not for the first time, he found her presence...unnerving, he supposed it was. Aside from the attraction thing, that was. Because it was like she was always "on," practically crackling with energy. Made sense, he supposed, given her being a drama teacher. But the idea of being around that all the time—especially considering the little life-suckers his kids were—made Ethan very tired. Merri... She'd been the epitome of calm. Not dull, no, but steady. Soothing.

Grief twinged, just enough to prod awake the loneliness, usually smothered under blankets of busyness and obligation. Willing it go back to sleep, Ethan walked over to the fireplace, figuring he might as well stack wood for this evening's fire as the house filled with the scents of bacon and cinnamon rolls. Jules was going all out. Great.

"I wouldn't know peaceful if it bit me in the butt," Ethan finally said, to fill the void as much as anything. Crouching, he grabbed a couple of logs from the metal bucket next to the hearth. "There were always a lot of kids around when I was growing up. I was one of five, four of us being adopted."

"Five? Wow."

"And my parents fostered probably two dozen more over the years."

"No kidding? That's awesome."

His back to Claire, Ethan smiled as he arranged the logs in the firebox. "Yeah," he said, getting to his feet and dusting off his hands. "They were something else."

Wearing an easy smile, Claire leaned against the arm of the sofa, her arms crossed, looking less…crackly. "Were?"

"Well, Pop still is, although he's more than content being a grandpa these days. Mom passed away some years back. But being raised with all those kids… It only seemed natural that I'd have a batch of my own someday. Would've had more, but that wasn't in the cards—"

And why the hell was he blathering on to this woman he barely knew? But while he could stanch the blathering, he couldn't do a blamed thing about the memories—of the other babies he and Merri had lost…of what he'd lost, period. Of the what-might-have-beens he rarely indulged, for everyone's sake. And yet—stronger, even, than the scents coming from the kitchen—they practically choked him this morning. It was strange how even after more than three years they could pounce out of nowhere, throw him for a loop.

Releasing a breath, he met Claire's disconcertingly gentle gaze again and switched the subject. "You got brothers and sisters?"

"Nope," she said, shaking her head before plopping cross-legged on the floor to rub Barney's belly. "There were a few distant cousins, but I rarely saw them." She grinned when the dog licked her hand. "I like people. It's *living* with them I have issues with. I have a cat, though. Does that count?"

"I'm gonna have to say no to that," Ethan said, and Claire snorted another little laugh as the dog crawled into her lap.

"What is he?"

"A schnoodle." Claire's eyes lifted to his. "Schnauzer/poodle. We got him…" He cleared his throat. "Three years ago."

Still petting the dog, Claire quietly said, "Juliette really keeps trying to fix you up?"

"Yeah," he breathed out.

"I assume you've asked her to back off?"

"Repeatedly. Only to get this look like I'm speaking Klingon—"

"Breakfast's ready!" Jules called, and Claire shoved to her feet again.

"I could talk to her, if you want—"

"I can handle my own daughter, thanks," Ethan snapped, only to realize how dumb that sounded, considering what he'd said not two seconds before. A realization Claire obviously picked up on, judging from the damn twinkle in her eyes.

"Yeah, well, as someone who used to *be* a teenage girl I can tell you they're very good at ignoring what they don't want to hear. Especially from their fathers. And since this doesn't only concern you, I do reserve the right to set things straight from my end."

Jeez, the woman was worse than his daughter. But Ethan also guessed she had Juliette's ear, which apparently he didn't. At least not about this.

"Fine. Do whatever you think is best. But for now… let's just get this breakfast over with, okay?"

"Sure thing," Claire said with a quick smile before following him to the kitchen, and Ethan pushed out another sigh that, God willing, in a half hour this—she—would be nothing more than a tiny blip on the old radar screen.

Because it'd taken the entire three years since Merri's death to fine-tune the playbook that held his family, his life, together...and damned if he was gonna let some curly-headed cutie distract him from it now.

Claire ducked into the main floor half bath as the land-line rang: Jules had already picked up by the time Ethan reached the kitchen, deftly cradling it between her jaw and her shoulder as she served up omelets and fried potatoes, looking so much like her mother Ethan's heart knocked.

"Hey, Baba—" The spatula hovering over the skillet, she went stock-still. "Oh, no...that sucks! Ick....Yeah, I'll tell him....No, we'll work it out," she said as Ethan motioned for her to give him the phone. But she only brandished the spatula, shaking her head. "Of course I'm sure. You need us for anything?...Okay, then....We'll talk later." She redocked the phone, glancing at Ethan as she finished dishing up breakfast. "Baba's got a tummy bug, she can't take Bella to dance class."

He silently swore. Right or wrong, he depended on Merri's parents to sometimes fill the gap, a role they both seemed to relish. And it'd been Carmela's idea to put the little jumping bean in ballet class to burn off at least some of her boundless energy. Kid could run ten circles around her brothers. Speaking of whom... "The boys have their game at ten, I can't do both."

"Another argument for letting me get my license sooner rather than later—"

"Forget it. Maybe I could get Pop to take her—"

"PopPop in a room full of baby ballerinas. Yeah, I can totally see that. Hey—maybe Miss Jacobs could do it?"

"Maybe Miss Jacobs could do what?" Claire said as she returned, scrubbing her obviously still-damp hands across her butt.

Ethan looked away. "And I'm sure she has better things to do with her morning."

"And you always *say,* Dad, it never hurts to ask. Right? Anyway, sit, both of you, everything's ready. So Bella has ballet this morning," she went on as Claire sat, "and my grandmother usually takes her, 'cause the boys have football or soccer or whatever—it's always something. Only she's sick and can't do it. So I said maybe you could. It's not far, right over on Main—"

"Omigosh—not Miss Louise's?"

"Yeah. You know it?"

"Know it? I took classes there for more than ten years! She's still alive?"

"Barely, but yeah—"

And naturally, Bella picked that moment to bounce into the kitchen in her pink tights and black leotard. "Is Baba here yet? 'Cause I'm all ready, see? And can I have a piece of bacon?"

"Help yourself," Jules said, holding the plate out for her sister as Ethan said, "You're not supposed to leave for an hour yet. But in any case—"

"Your grandmother's not feeling well," Claire said, chomping the end off her own piece of bacon, "so I'm going to take you."

Ethan's brows slammed together. "What?"

"My morning's free, so why not? Besides, I've always been a sucker for trips down memory lane. So what do you say, Isabella?"

That got the Very Concerned Face. "But I don't know you. And Baba always takes me for lunch afterward."

"It's okay, Belly," Jules said, "Ms. Jacobs is one of my teachers, she's cool—"

"And maybe Juliette could go with us, if that would make you feel better," Claire said, adding, at the teen's nod, "and we can still go to lunch after."

"Promise?"

"Promise." Then she grinned at her breakfast. "Even though I probably won't be hungry for hours. This looks amazing, Juliette."

"Thanks," she said, then shot Ethan a grin that sent a brief, sharp pain shooting through his skull.

Chapter Two

Nostalgia swelled through Claire the instant Isabella shoved open the door to the storefront studio, releasing a cloud of steam heat permeated with the tang of rosin and sweat, Miss Louise's too-sweet perfume. For her entire childhood, this was the scent of Saturday mornings, and it made her smile.

"Um…we can't stay," Juliette said after Bella raced into a dressing room overflowing with squealing little girls.

"Oh, I know." Because the presence of parents and such, except at recitals, tended to either make little Pavlova wannabes painfully self-conscious or turn them into obnoxious show-offs. "I just want to say hello. For old time's sake."

"Meet me outside, then?"

"You bet."

Because when an opportunity plunks into your lap, you take it. Of course, Ethan could simply be misreading Juliette's natural friendliness for machinations of the matchmaking kind. Certainly the idea had never occurred to

Claire, even after the girl invited her for breakfast. But if Ethan's hunch was right, then the sooner this was all put to rest, the better. For everyone's sake.

Especially Ethan's, Claire thought as the girl wandered off to window-shop, and Claire remembered the pressure Mom's well-meaning friends had put on her after Claire's dad died to get out there and date again. As well as her mother emphatically telling them to mind their own business, Norman was irreplaceable, end of discussion.

So obviously that's how it was for some people—you only got one shot at love, and when it was over, it was over. True, Ethan was a lot younger, and she knew widowers were more likely to remarry than widows. But still. Bad enough the poor guy had to endure the merciless flirtations of every unattached female teacher at Hoover. So if Juliette *was* trying to set him up… So wrong—

"Oh, my God—Claire Jacobs?"

Green eyes sparkling over powder-caked cheeks, Miss Louise floated across the worn wood floor in pink ballet slippers and a wispy chiffon skirt probably older than Claire. After a brief, fierce hug, bloodred lips pursed as the redhead gave Claire a once-over that would make a Mafia goon cringe. "What on earth are you doing here, doll? I thought you'd blown this joint years ago."

"I had. But I'm back. Teaching up at Hoover. Drama and English," she said to the woman's raised, insect leg–like eyebrows.

"You don't say?" Her sharp gaze darted over a dozen spinning, chattering little girls. "Which one's yours?"

"Isabella. But only for this morning."

"Bella, yeah. Little blonde toughie. Love her to bits." Miss Louise lowered her voice. "So sad about her mommy, but the kid seems to be doing okay. So…wait a minute…" Her eyes sidled to Claire's. "You and her daddy…?"

"No," Claire said, laughing, and the microthin brows

arched again. "Long story, I'm only pinch-hitting. Anyway, figured I'd say hi." She hitched her bag onto her shoulder. "How long's the class?"

"Forty-five minutes." Her mouth curved. "You can still do a double pirouette?"

"Ha! Like I ever could!"

Miss Louise grinned, then patted her arm. "Hey, we have an adult class on Wednesday evenings. Lots of mommies who took ballet when they were kids, now they want to lose the baby weight." Smirking, she glanced at Claire's midsection. "Couldn't hurt, right?"

"It's the vest, I swear!"

"Whatever," she said, walking away. "Ten bucks a class, starts at seven on the dot…"

Okay, so maybe she'd put on a few pounds since she moved back, Claire thought on a sigh as she left the studio. And maybe—she saw Juliette staring at something in the window a few stores down—there were more important things to worry about.

She hustled down the street, which in three weeks would be all gussied up for Christmas. Right now, though, despite all the redbrick fronts and colorful awnings and pretty black iron benches—the little town was nothing if not determined to survive the plague that was urban sprawl—between the stripped-bare maples and barren planters lining the curbs, it was kind of blah.

And fricking freezing, the stiff river breeze ripping right through her vest. She dug her hat out of her pocket and crammed it over her curls, but that wasn't going to help her soon-to-be-numb butt. In contrast, Juliette—who was hardly dressed like a Laplander—seemed totally unfazed by the bitter wind, her streaked hair whipping around her face as she stared.

"Wh-whatcha l-looking at?"

She pointed. "Aren't they the cutest things ever?"

"They" being a pair of fluff-ball kittens, one gold, one gray, wrestling in a shredded paper nest in the window of the local adoption shelter's adoption center.

"Omigosh…" Suddenly her bum didn't feel so cold. "Adorable."

"Dad said maybe Belly could have a kitten for Christmas, if she promises to take care of it. Meaning I'll probably end up doing it. Like I do everything else…" She gave her head a sharp shake. "Sorry," she mumbled, still watching the kittens. "That sounds terrible."

"No, it doesn't," Claire said gently, steeling herself for wherever the conversation might be headed. "It sounds like somebody who's got a lot on her plate these days. Totally understandable."

"Except it's not even true, not really. Yeah, okay, so sometimes it does feel like that, but it's not like Dad doesn't do more than his share. Speaking of having a lot on his plate—he's got his teaching, and coaching, and making sure the boys don't, like, destroy the house. Or themselves," she added with a little smile, then sighed. "And it's not like I mind cooking. Actually, I love it. And we got this new washer/dryer set last year, it's so awesome, it does everything but fold. And Baba helps, too, when she can. Except there's only so much she can do. Because she's, like, *sixty*…" Juliette looked over, her brow knotting at Claire's gotta-keep-the-blood-moving jig. "You cold?"

"A l-little, yeah."

"There's that tearoom over there, maybe we could get some hot chocolate or something while we're waiting?"

"You're on."

The two-bit diner Claire dimly remembered from her childhood had morphed into something very quaint and prissy, but the hot chocolate came in enormous mugs with a mountain of whipped cream, so she was good. She would have been even better with one of the pastries winking at her from underneath the gleaming glass dome on the counter, but remembering the brutal look Miss Louise had given her hips, she passed.

"That was so nice, you offering to take Belly to dance class," Juliette said, focused on her mug as she swiped a napkin over her whipped-cream mustache. "I'm sure Dad appreciated it."

"No biggie. Glad I could help."

"So it was a good thing we ran into each other at the estate sale, huh? And then you taking me home? Like…it was fate or something."

Claire's lips twitched. *"Serendipity."*

"Exactly." Juliette leaned forward, her eyes all blue fire, and Claire thought, *And here it comes.* "Don't you ever think that things happen for a reason? Sometimes, anyway. Like there's some big plan for each of us, if we can only see it?"

Claire sat straighter in her chair, a pink, curlicued confection that was hell on her back. "I certainly think life presents…opportunities," she said carefully. "But being open to opportunity is very different from seeing something that's not actually there. Or trying to make something happen." She met the girl's gaze dead on. "No matter how right it might feel to *you*."

The girl sagged back in her own chair, hugging her mug to her chest. "Dad said something, didn't he?"

"Even if he hadn't, I would've figured it out on my own." *Eventually. Maybe.* Juliette snorted. "So you have been trying to fix him up?"

"No! Well, okay, sort of. I mean…" She blew out a sigh. "What's wrong with wanting him to be *open* to the possibility of getting married again? Or at least having a girlfriend."

"Because that's for him to decide, sweetie. Not you. Sometimes, when someone we love isn't…around anymore—"

"Mom died, Miss Jacobs. It's okay, you can say it. She *died*. And it sucks, and we were all miserable, and I know Dad still is, but..." She shook her head. "I know it sounds like I'm only thinking about myself, but I'm not, I swear. The extra work's not that big a deal, and like I said, I'm cool with cooking. And I love my brothers and sister, even when they're being pains. Except, for one thing, I've only got three more years before I'm gone. Because I'm so not sticking around for college. Not if I can help it. And for another..."

Juliette set her mug back down. "You didn't know Dad before. When he was happy. I'm not saying he acted like a clown all the time or anything—that's not his style— but at least he smiled, you know? I mean, for real. Eyes and everything. And laughed... Omigosh, his laugh... It was insane."

Claire took a sip of her drink. "Having a hard time picturing that."

"I'm having a hard time *remembering* it. Which is so sad." The girl sighed, then scooped up a blob of whipped cream with her finger, poked it in her mouth. "I do remember, though, how he used to look at Mom when she didn't know he was watching, and he'd, like, *glow*. Seriously. Like he'd struck gold or something. And that feeling... You'd walk into the house, and you'd just feel it, that glow. Like everything was okay. And it's not there anymore." She looked up, tears brimming. "And I can't believe that's how it's supposed to be for the rest of our lives. Especially the rest of D-Dad's."

"Oh, honey..." Claire reached for the teen's hand, her heart aching in spite of herself. Yes, the thought niggled that the girl might be manipulating her—or trying to—but something louder said that wasn't what was going on here. Whether Claire fully understood or not Juliette's reasons for confiding in her, that wasn't the issue. The issue was that the child really was hurting, and for her dad more than for herself. That put a whole different spin on things, one she wondered if Ethan even realized. "Your heart's in the right place, wanting someone to fill the gap in your lives. Especially your dad's. But as I said, you can't force these things to happen. If you father's not ready—"

"But how does he know that if he won't even try? It's been more than three years already!"

"And I know, for you, that feels like a long time. For your dad, it might feel like no time at all." She let go. "You know, not every kid in your situation is down with getting a new parent. In fact, many are absolutely horrified by the idea—"

"And you don't think I'm not? Hey, I *devoured* fairy tales when I was little—all those wicked stepmothers?" She shuddered. "Serious nightmare material. So yeah, while I think things would be much better if Dad found someone else…" Her face pinked. "I don't totally trust him to pick for himself."

A startled laugh popped out of Claire's mouth. "So you've decided to prescreen applicants for the position?"

"Seemed like a good idea."

"And I'm on your short list."

"Well…yeah," Juliette said, and Claire laughed again. "Why?"

"Because you're *sane?*"

"Spoken like someone who clearly doesn't know me very well."

"Oh, trust me. I know from insanity. Not to mention desperation. At least you don't go around shoving your boobs in guys' faces."

Claire smiled. "This is true. But, honey, I'm not your mother—"

"Duh, I know that—"

"No, what I mean is… Okay, let's get real. Setting aside

the fact that I'm no more interested in your dad than he is in me—"

"And maybe if you guys got to know each other—"

"Juliette—stop. Even if, by some very, *very* slim chance, your dad and I hit it off, it takes a special person to take on a ready-made family. And trust me, I'm not that person."

"But—"

She lifted a hand to stop whatever the girl was about to say. "*Four* kids? And while I might be able to fake it with girls…your brothers? No way."

"But…you obviously like kids—"

"I love them. Teaching them, though. Not raising them. I was an only child, honey. I'm doing well to keep a cat and two houseplants alive. Sweetie," she said, "whatever's best for you guys… It'll happen. When it's supposed to and without your…help. After all, your dad picked your mom on his own, right?"

Finally, the wind seemed to go out of the girl's sails. "Guess I hadn't thought of that." Then she sighed. "But it's so…hard."

"I know, honey. Really." Claire glanced up at the clock over the counter, dug her wallet out of her purse. "And we need to pick up your sister."

Juliette fell silent after that. Until, right as they reached the dance studio, she said, "Can we at least be friends?"

"Of course! You need someone to talk to, I'm here. But you need to tell your dad your matchmaking days are over. Because he doesn't need to worry about that on top of everything else. Deal?"

"Deal," Juliette said on a gusty sigh as her little sister burst outside, and she squatted to hug her.

So, whew, done, Claire thought after she took the kids for burgers and shakes, staying in the car after driving them home. But listening to Isabella's giggles as they ate,

Juliette's too-grown-up observations about her world... It hadn't exactly been horrible.

And you know what else? Seeing the little one streak to her father, who was outside raking the last of the leaves, watching him scoop her into his arms, his eyes glued to hers as she relayed every detail of the past two hours... Having someone like that in her life might not be so horrible, either. Except there were way too many ifs and buts and excepts attached to that thought to even go there. Because if Claire had learned anything from her over-before-it-began marriage, it was that serious relationships required at least a certain level of self-sacrifice—something she didn't seem very good at.

And this man—he glanced over with a nod and mouthed *Thanks,* and she nodded back before putting the car in Reverse—after what he'd been through?

Whatever he needed, Claire definitely wasn't it.

Juliette fell back on her bed, making poor Barney jump, then pick his way across the rumpled Marimekko comforter to slather Juliette's face with sloppy kisses.

"Stop, *stop!*" she squealed, trying to squirm away from the wriggling dog. Sprawled on the extra twin bed a few feet away, Rosie Valencia, her bestie since forever, laughed her not-exactly-small butt off.

"Get her, Barney!" Rosie cheered, which only made the stupid dog lick faster. "Maybe you can wash away that rotten mood."

"Why does everybody keep *saying* that?" Juliette said, shoving the dog off her chest to haul herself upright in the field of giant red-and-hot-pink flowers. She'd thought this was the coolest bedding ever when she'd been ten and Mom had surprised her with the makeover that banished the cutesy Winnie-the-Pooh stuff of her childhood. And it wasn't that she hated it, exactly. But it was time for a change, maybe.

The dog flopped over, baring his pink belly. Sighing, Juliette obliged, which of course made him crunch forward to madly lick her hand. "I'm not in a bad mood," she muttered.

"Uh-huh." Rosie swept her nearly black hair over her shoulder as she shifted on the bed, her math book open on her lap. Pale green eyes, eerie against Rosie's dark skin, met Juliette's. Like her, Rosie was also the eldest. Only she had *six* siblings. All boys. As crazy as it got here, it was ten times worse at Rosie's. "So you gonna tell me why you're pissed, or what?"

Even two days later it still stung that she had to admit Miss Jacobs was right—that whatever was gonna happen, or not, Juliette couldn't influence it one way or the other. Unfortunately, this flew in the face not only of everything Mom had ever said about people being in charge of their own destiny, but of Juliette's naturally impatient nature.

Something she doubted Rosie, who was the most laid-back person ever, would understand. The upside to this was that nine times out of ten Rosie was like "sure, whatever" about pretty much anything Juliette suggested. Theirs was definitely a symbiotic relationship. But being from a family in which everybody apparently lived to some ridiculous age—she had a great-grandmother who was like a hundred and five, yeesh—Rosie couldn't possibly understand the huge honking hole inside Juliette that only seemed to grow larger every day. Instead of closing up, like you'd expect. Like she'd hoped.

"It's just...stuff," she said, grabbing her own math book and loose-leaf binder from the foot of the bed, smacking both open. "I'll deal. So...what did you think of the cast choices for the holiday play?"

Some Dr. Seuss version of *A Christmas Carol.* Hysterical. And it had a gazillion parts, so lots of kids could be in it. Even if for only a few minutes. Like her and Rosie. Because lead roles only went to juniors and seniors.

"They all sounded okay during the read-through, I guess," Rosie said. "Although I'd like to swat that smarmy smile off whatshername's face." Juliette smiled, knowing exactly who Rosie meant. Amber Fortunato. Big hair, bigger boobs, Daddy owned a BMW dealership. 'Nuff said. "But her boyfriend? The dude who's playing Scrooge's nephew? What's his name?"

Juliette's cheeks prickled. "Scott Jenkins?" she said, staring really hard at the first problem. She'd paid attention in class, honest to God, but she still didn't get it.

"Yeah, Scott. He is so frickin' cute. I could totally lick ice cream from those dimples. And those blue eyes… *Le* sigh."

Honestly. Whatever popped into Rosie's head slid right out of her mouth a second later. Juliette might be impatient, but she wasn't impulsive. She did think things through before she said/did them. Mostly.

"He's a junior," she said, still staring at the book. Still blushing. "Out of our league. Not to mention, hello? Amber?"

"Please. I give that two weeks, tops." Rosie tilted her head. "And you do know your face is about the same color as those flowers, right?"

"Shut. Up."

"So you should totally ask him out."

Juliette's eyes slid to Rosie's.

"Okay, so in two weeks. When my prediction proves true."

"Right. Because even if Scott didn't laugh in my face, Dad would kill me. And then him, for accepting. Then me again, to make sure I got the point."

"So what if he asked *you* out? You know, after he and

Amber split and he's all looking for someone to heal his wounds and stuff."

Juliette sighed. Because as much as she hated to admit it, that particular fantasy had crossed her mind a time or twenty. But still... "Slightly different order, same outcome. We'd both be dead. You know I can't date yet, Rosie. Not until I'm sixteen. And in any case..." She glared at the book again. Nope, not making any more sense than it did five minutes ago. "I've got too much else on my mind right now."

"Like what?"

"Like passing geometry, for one thing."

"So get a tutor. And for another?"

Juliette blew a slow breath through her nose. Yeah, Miss Jacobs had said she could talk to her anytime, and Juliette knew she meant it. But when, exactly, would that happen? At school? And anyway, their previous conversation hadn't actually solved anything, had it—?

"Jules?" her dad said, knocking at the partly open door. His face looked pinched, like always. "Dinner's ready in ten minutes. You staying, Rosie?"

"If it's okay...?"

"Carmela brought over a tuna casserole. There's enough for half the town."

Rosie giggled. "I'll ask my mom, but sure. Thanks."

Dad left the door ajar like before, the floor creaking underneath the carpet as he walked away. Rosie's eyes cut to Juliette's before she leaned forward and whispered, "Is your dad okay? He looks exhausted."

"So it's not my imagination."

"No... Oh. You're worried about him, huh?"

Juliette supposed it was normal for a kid who's lost a parent to worry more about the one who's left. So she nodded, then basically repeated what she'd said to Miss Jacobs on Saturday—with a few adjustments to cover her butt—

and Rosie got this totally understanding look on her face, a lot like when she'd heard Juliette's mom had died, and she'd come right over and they'd hugged for like ten minutes, crying their eyes out. Rosie might have her shallow moments, but they'd been friends for so long for a reason.

Her friend sighed. "I can't imagine how Papi would cope without Mama. Speaking of which…" She dug her phone out of her purse, texted her mother. "She's, like, his life. And yeah, she says I can stay. But…I have…to help with the dishes." She rolled her eyes, then texted a two-letter reply, returned her attention to Juliette. "You do know you can't fix this, right? That it's your dad's life?"

"Pretty much what Miss Jacobs said—"

"Omigod—" Rosie sucked in a breath, then lowered her voice. "*Please* don't tell me you tried fixing up them up? God, Jules, Miss Elliot was bad enough, but Miss Jacobs? Seriously?"

"Okay, setting aside that we all agree I shouldn't be trying to fix up Dad with anybody—"

"Ya think?"

"—what's wrong with Miss Jacobs?"

"Her? Not a thing. She's one of the coolest teachers ever. But have you met your father, *chica*? He's a good man, don't get me wrong—and he's a hottie, too—"

"Jeez, Rosie, boundaries."

"Hey. These eyes, they know what they see. But I can't imagine two people more wrong for each other. Don't forget, I remember your mom. She and Miss Jacobs… Like two different species. Think about it—she's all bubbly and goofy and whatnot, and your dad's…not. And neither was your mom. Get real, Jules—"

"It's okay, I'm over it. My matchmaking days are done."

"You swear?"

Juliette crossed her heart. "It's just…" She flopped back on the bed again. Barney belly-crawled over to lay his chin on her stomach. "It's Christmas coming, you know? Mom... She loved everything about it, practically turned herself inside out to make sure it was great. The baking, the decorations, the way Christmas carols were always playing..."

"I remember. This was always, like, the coolest house on the block." Rosie snorted. "My poor mom, she does well to remember to buy those sucky grocery store cookies. Not that the boys care—if it's sugarfied, they'll eat it."

"Same here," Juliette said with a tight grin, then blew out a shaky breath. "Even after I figured out Santa wasn't real, Mom still made it magic somehow. Sure, I can make cookies and decorate and put on those old CDs and stuff. Except it's not the same. It's like..." She turned to Rosie. "Like she took the magic with her."

"I get why you think that, Jules," Rosie said, her eyes all kind. "I do. But to say the magic died with her?" She shook her head, hard, making her curls shiver. "That's stupid."

"Gee, thanks."

"It's true. I mean, sure, your mom might've expressed the magic, but it's not like she owned it or anything. Because it's all around us. *In* all of us—"

Dad called them for dinner; her friend pushed her books aside, then hoisted herself to her feet, brushing cookie crumbs off her expansive chest. "My *abuelita* always says, the more you try to tell the universe what you want, the harder it is to see what the universe is already trying to give you. We don't have to make stuff happen. We only have to *let* it."

"Wow. Deep."

"Hey, I've been listening to this crap my entire life. It was bound to come out of my mouth eventually."

Juliette laughed. Rosie could make her as mad as all get-out, but she could always make her feel better, too. And deep down, she knew Rosie—or her grandmother—was right: she was going to have to be patient. To trust. And okay, to maybe dig a little deeper to find the magic inside herself, or at least to look harder for it. But as they went down to the kitchen, and she saw the strain tugging at her dad's mouth, heard the flatness in his voice, it occurred to her that, if she were still little enough to believe in Santa, she knew exactly what she'd ask him for.

Chapter Three

Seated at the dinged metal desk taking up nearly half the tiny office near the locker rooms, Ethan propped his hands behind his head, yawning so widely his ears popped. The overhead fluorescent light flickered, then settled back into the mesmeric one-note hum that inevitably lulled Ethan to sleep. Practice had ended a half hour ago, right before the sun whisked away its last feeble rays, leaving a bleak, damp cold in its wake. Possibility of light snow, they said. Ethan's knee protested, offering an unwelcome second opinion.

The silence this time of day... He hated it. Mainly because he could hear his own thoughts much too clearly. He glanced at the PE tests he was grading, blowing out a breath before shuffling the papers into a neat pile and stuffing them into his leather briefcase—Merri's present that first Christmas after he'd started teaching. Since he'd made a promise—to himself, to the kids, to Merri on the day of her funeral—to let nothing interfere with family time, he wasn't a fan of taking schoolwork home. But Jules, whose rehearsal would have ended two hours ago, was probably more than ready to be relieved by this point. As capable as she was at handling the boys and Bella, that wasn't her job. So—he yawned again—he'd finish up the grading after the younger ones went to bed, while Jules was doing her own homework.

The movement sent another paper on the end of the desk fluttering to the linoleum floor below. Ethan bent to retrieve it, puffing out another breath. A notice from the office that two of his best players' grades were jeopardizing their positions on the team. Ethan rubbed his eyes, then squinted at the names. Roland White and Zach Baker, both juniors, both in imminent danger of failing English III.

With Claire Jacobs.

Ethan almost laughed. Didn't that figure? The good news was, it was still early enough to turn things around, at least for next year. The bad news was, they had to bring up their grades, fast, or be cut from the team for the rest of the season. And that would not be good. For a boatload of reasons.

But not a damned thing he could do about it right now.

He zipped up his Hoover Hawks jacket against the icy cold as the heavy metal door clanged shut behind him, trapping the silence inside…if not the memories. Despite the facelift the school had gotten since his own student days, every time he set foot in this place he imagined a grinning Merri sashaying down the tiled hallway in her blue-and-white cheerleading uniform, her blond hair pulled into bouncing, twin ponytails. Hell, yes, he thought as he trudged to his Explorer on the far side of the faculty lot, they'd been the stereotype "perfect" couple, the cheerleader and the star quarterback…except there'd been nothing typical about the girl who'd knocked the wind clean out of him from the moment he saw her—

Footsteps crunching behind him made him whip around, immediately on guard—a permanently ingrained habit from his time in Afghanistan.

"Sorry," Claire said, appearing like an apparition in front of him. "Didn't mean to spook you." She nodded toward her car, parked in the one spot the halogen lights didn't reach. "I'm right over there."

He remembered White and Baker, that he needed to discuss their grades with her. Except it was cold, and late, and he not only needed to get home but to line up his ducks before broaching the subject. He'd had these conversations before, with other teachers about other players, and they didn't always go so well. So he needed a minute or two to gather his thoughts, plan a strategy. Tomorrow would be soon enough. So he waved, expecting her to continue on to the sedate, middle-aged white sedan he was guessing she had not picked out herself.

Instead, she came closer. He frowned, still cautious, his heart thumping a little harder than usual. Okay, it'd be a lie to say she hadn't occasionally popped into his head in the past week and a half, especially after Juliette had told him about her and Claire's little chat. It would also be a lie to say he didn't sometimes catch himself half hoping their paths would cross, if only to get a glimpse of that smile. Those glittering brown eyes. Like a spark of warmth in a cold, barren landscape. And lie *número tres* would be that, caution aside, he wasn't completely unhappy about her appearance now, even if only because right now he'd welcome almost any excuse to escape from his own head.

Although, since Claire *was* inside his head—taking up way more real estate than was prudent...

Hell.

"What are *you* doing here so late?" Ethan said, aiming for friendly but detached. Instead of, you know, slightly deranged. "Juliette said rehearsal was over at four."

"It was. Then I had lesson planning," Claire said in that voice he now realized reminded him of a very dry martini. Something else he hadn't had in a long while. "If I don't do it here, it doesn't get done. And I suck at improv." Her hands jammed into the pockets of her big puffy purple coat—she wore a backpack, like one of the kids—she quietly laughed, her loose curls dancing around her face. "Both onstage and in the classroom. You seriously drive the four blocks from your house?"

"When it's twenty degrees at six forty-five in the morning, yes." He wasn't about to tell her the real reason, that the cold was brutal on his bum knee, even with the brace. Because whining was for losers.

"Gotcha," Claire said, removing her hands to wrap the coat—she looked like a cross between the Michelin Man and the Fruit of the Loom grapes—more tightly around herself. "So you haven't seen Juliette, I take it? In the past hour, I mean?"

"No. She always goes right home so her grandmother can get back to *her* home." His mouth pulled to one side. "We have a system. A complicated one, but it works."

"I can imagine. Well, I won't keep you," she said, smiling, and Ethan almost felt something thaw inside him. Almost. Until she said, "But Juliette is probably going to be very excited when you get there."

"Oh? About what?"

"I'll let her tell you," she said, then started toward her car, taking the warmth with her, and suddenly he didn't want her to leave. Not yet.

"She told me about your conversation," he called after her. Already at her car, she turned.

"What conver— Oh. You mean from the morning I took the little one to dance class?"

He nodded, feeling the rims of his ears start to burn from the cold. And maybe something more. "Yeah. I should have said something before. To thank you, I mean. She promised… She said she was out of the matchmaking business. For me, anyway."

Claire walked back a few steps, clearly trying to keep her teeth from chattering. "Good. Considering I did everything short of making her sign an affidavit. In blood."

Ethan's cheeks hurt when he tried to smile. Because it was so cold. "You have the magic touch."

She humphed. "Hardly. But I do remember what fifteen felt like, when my entire life could be summed up in one word—*yearning.*"

"For what?"

A short, choked sound pushed through her lips. "Oh, God. Everything. Or at least, everything I felt was being unfairly kept out of my reach. Cool clothes. A boyfriend. Straight hair," she added with a smirk, and Ethan's cheeks ached again. "The difference is, though, that I never had the chutzpah to actually do something about my discontent. Well, except for the hair, but we won't go there. Juliette… Yeah, she might overreach, but at least she's reaching. And the thing is…she's not reaching for herself. Not about this, anyway."

"What…what do you mean?"

Claire stuffed her hands into her pockets again, her skin sallow in the ugly bright light. Despite her height— or lack thereof—there was nothing even remotely delicate about her, Ethan realized. Good thing, since many of her students were a lot taller than she was.

"I don't know Juliette that well, of course," she said. Cautiously, he thought. "And I certainly don't know you, what's going on in your head. But I do know what it's like, to lose a parent. The empty feeling that leaves in your heart. And how much you wish…" Briefly, she glanced away, then back at him. "All you want is to plug up that emptiness. But what struck me about Juliette is that it's not only *her* heart she wants to plug up. It's yours. The matchmaking... She only wants you to be happy again."

Ethan started. "She thinks I'm not happy?"

"Apparently so. And for a teenager in the throes of adolescent self-involvement? That kind of empathy is pretty remarkable. Which says to me she's got a remarkable dad. And criminy, it's getting late, I'm so sorry—"

She hustled back to her car before Ethan could even begin to figure out what to say, only to turn around again. "Oh! I almost forgot—I got a notice from the office about those two players of yours in my sixth period class? We need to talk."

"Uh, yeah. We do. When's your prep period?"

"First."

"Mine, too."

"So." She grinned. "Your place or mine?"

"Mine," he said, wanting to be on his own turf. "Room 110, right behind the gym."

"Got it," she said, then climbed in her car and took off, leaving Ethan to realize his aching knee was the least of his problems.

As usual, all four kids accosted him the instant he set foot inside the house, yammering about their days. Also as usual, he swept Bella into his arms to get a hug and kiss, and as usual, she made a face about his pokey end-of-day beard. And the twins were doing their speaking-in-tandem thing about something that had happened at school, and Juliette was telling them all to go wash their hands, dinner was almost ready, and he thought that while this obviously wasn't the life he'd envisioned, it was the life he had, and he was determined to keep that life on as even a keel as humanly possible.

Then Claire's words about his being remarkable—there

was a laugh—smacked him upside the head, and for a moment everything tilted again.

"Dad?" Juliette said, setting a huge bowl of spaghetti and meatballs in the middle of the table as the others scampered off to wash up. "You okay?"

Finally he looked at his oldest child, noticed how much she was beaming. "Yeah, baby, I'm fine. Wow, this looks great. Did you make this, or your grandmother?"

"Baba brought over the meatballs, I made the sauce. There's salad and garlic bread, too—"

"So I ran into Miss Jacobs in the parking lot, and she said you had some big news to tell me?"

The kid's smile punched him right in the gut, like it always did. "The girl playing the Ghost of Christmas Past had to drop out of the play, so Miss Jacobs had a bunch of us read for it. Then the rest of the cast voted on who should get the part, and...I won!"

"Way to go, you!" he said, giving her a high five...even if his enthusiasm didn't match hers. And yes, he felt bad about that, that he couldn't get completely behind something that clearly meant so much to his daughter.

Whose eyes were sparkling more than he'd ever seen them. "I mean, I know it's only a high school play, but I so wanted this—I even prayed about it."

Ethan felt his mouth flatten. "Jules..."

"Oh, I didn't ask God to give me the part! But I didn't think it'd hurt to ask Him to help me do my best when I read. That's okay, right? I mean, isn't that how the guys pray before the game? To play their best?"

She had him there. Granted, the prayers were unofficial and unsanctioned—and completely voluntary—but the pregame ritual had been an open secret for years. Maple River was a town of many faiths, and a surprising number of the kids walked the walk. And if praying fired the guys up, made them more focused, Ethan was all for it. So he turned a blind eye, even if his own faith had been a little tattered around the edges for some time.

"Not that I'm any expert," he said, "but seeing as it worked, I guess you got it right."

"I am so excited," she said on a blissful sigh, turning away to collect bowls from the cupboard. "Because it's, like, another step, right?"

"Toward?"

The bowls clunked onto the table. "My acting career, what else?"

"And like you said…it's only a high school play."

"Dad," she said, giving him the side eye as she clunked the bowls on the table. "Have you not been listening to anything I've been saying for the past three months? I *love* acting. It's like…it's like I've finally figured out who I am. What I'm supposed to do with my life. And yes, I know I've done like a million other things before now, and given up on all of them, but…but this is different."

Ethan's forehead knotted. "I thought your eBay business…?"

"That's part of my plan, yeah. To help pay my way through college. But I already know I want to major in drama. And not at some Podunk local school, either. At Yale. Or Carnegie Mellon. Maybe even Julliard."

At that, a tremor traipsed up his spine, the same tremor—or one of its many, many cousins—that had assailed him with relentless regularity ever since Merri's death, the realization that he couldn't protect the kids from making mistakes, from disappointment.

It wasn't that he didn't want Jules to be happy—of course he did. Hell, he'd sell his own soul—presuming the market value on it hadn't tanked—to ensure all of his kids' happiness. That was a given. But worry niggled, too, that she was only setting herself up for a fall. Not only about being one of the few stagestruck kids to actually make it as an actor, but even getting into those schools…

Then reality clunked him on the noggin, reminding him again that Jules was only fifteen, that her only brush with acting was this class, which she'd only been in for a few months. With that, the fear backed off and went looking for someone else to torment. At least for the moment. Yeah, there was stuff he still wanted to say, warnings he wanted to give. But at this point, he'd only be wasting his breath, since what was the likelihood of a strong-willed teenage girl actually heeding her father's warnings?

So all he said was, "Those are some lofty goals," as the other kids stormed back into the kitchen to noisily take their places at the table.

"Aim high, Mom always said. Right?"

Actually, what she'd said was, "Aim high, kick fear in the nuts and live like you'll die tomorrow."

"Right," Ethan said, swallowing the baseball-size knot in his throat.

The next morning, Claire cautiously threaded through the herd of students surging to their first-period classes, the cardboard tray holding two coffees precariously clutched in her still-frozen fingers. It was ridiculous how badly her stomach was boogying, never mind that Ethan's office door would most likely stay open and this wasn't even remotely personal. This was about the kids, period. And surely she had the wherewithal to pull off a simple conference without sounding like someone who'd been teaching for five minutes.

Someone who, despite how far she'd come, was still far more comfortable on a stage or in the front of a classroom of rowdy students than she was one-on-one with the likes of Ethan Noble.

Gosh, she hadn't been on this side of the building since

those long-ago days of required PE in the tenth grade, a thought that did not evoke even the faintest trace of nostalgia. The bell rang, magically sucking students out of the halls and into classrooms. Claire scurried the rest of the way to Ethan's office, through halls that smelled faintly of chlorine from the indoor pool. His office door was open, but she rapped lightly on the glass insert, anyway. He glanced up, then stood, with what he probably thought was a smile.

"Hey," he said, looking as though he'd rather be anywhere else, with anyone else. Yeah, promised to be a great chat. "Right on time."

"I brought coffee," Claire said, holding aloft the tray, willing it not to wobble. "Couldn't remember what you liked, so I got straight black. Cream and sugar optional."

"Black's fine. Thanks."

Claire pried one of the cups out of its little nest, muttering a mild obscenity when a few drops squeezed out from underneath the lid and dribbled down the side. The tray clumsily lowered to his desk, she snatched a napkin from the bunch fortuitously wedged in one of the empty cutouts to wipe up her mess before handing the once-more-tidy cup to him.

"Thanks," Ethan said again as she wadded up the soggy napkin and stuffed it into her coat pocket. Looking almost amused, he reached behind him for a metal trash can, held it out.

"Right," she said, fishing out the napkin and dropping it into the receptacle. He replaced the can, then gestured toward the chair in front of his desk before sitting back in his, taking a long sip of the coffee. "Jules is very excited about getting that part, by the way."

Okay, good start... "And you didn't even hear the screech when the stage manager read her name. Like Justin Bieber had asked her out." Claire unsnapped her coat, took a drink of her own coffee. Still warm, hallelujah. "Or whoever the hottie du jour is, I'm not really up on these things."

"*You're* not up on these things." Ethan shook his head. "Do they change every week, or am I completely out of the loop?"

She smiled. "Both, probably," she said, and—amazingly—he started to smile back…only to apparently remember why they were there.

"So. We have an issue. About my players not passing your class."

"No," Claire said carefully. "Ultimately, this is Roland's and Zach's issue. Not ours. But I do want them to be successful. To *feel* successful—"

Ethan scowled. "And you think I don't?"

"In all areas of their lives. Not only football." She leaned forward, her heart hammering. That scowl… One might say it was intimidating. One might also say it was dead sexy, but this was neither the time nor the place. "Look, I'm well aware how important the football program is to Hoover. And that's fine…as far as it goes. The problem is, the guys get this idea that academics come a distant second to sports, especially *that* sport, that nothing trumps bringing home that dang championship trophy, that they're far more valued for their brawn than their brains. And for what? I care about these kids, Ethan. And it kills me to see them not even try to live up to their full potential. So…" She felt her face heat. "Thought I'd put that out there."

His silence seemed to suck the air out of the room, just as his steady gaze sucked the air from *her*. Then something flickered in those icy blue eyes, although his posture changed not one whit. "You like football?"

"Not particularly, no."

His mouth might've twitched. "You think it's stupid? Silly? Pointless?"

"Do I have to choose?"

"Good thing you brought coffee," Ethan said, and this time she definitely saw a twitch. "Otherwise a person might think you were here to pick a fight."

"Being up front isn't the same as picking a fight. But no way am I fudging grades so the kids can still play. Which I know other teachers have done."

At that, his brows lifted. Not a lot, but enough. "And you think I *asked* them to do that?"

"You tell me."

"No. Never."

"Oh."

"Yeah. *Oh.* Am I unhappy when I lose a good player because his grades suck? You bet. And I've never kept that a secret. Any more than I did when I was a student here, and I had to bust *my* buns to pass a couple of classes or risk getting cut from the team. I wasn't exactly academically gifted—or so I thought—so, yeah, I thought the policy was a load of crap. But if it eases your mind, I don't see it that way now."

"No?"

"No." The glimmer in his eyes faded. "Heck, nobody knows more than me that there's more to life than football," he said with a quiet intensity that riveted Claire's attention. "And that putting all your eggs in that particular basket is nothing but an invitation to watch all of 'em break. But try explaining that to a seventeen-year-old who's never known before what it feels like to be successful, to be *somebody,* before he discovered this one thing he's actually good at. Some of these guys, they can't see further ahead than next Friday night's game. Then there's the others who are looking to the future, who maybe need that game to clinch the championship, which in turn maybe'll snag the attention of a college scout. For them, football might be their only shot at actually going on to college—"

"Oh, come on, you've got players from pretty privileged backgrounds, too."

"True. But White and Baker aren't among them. I know these kids. Know their families, if they even have much of one. Hell, I went to school with some of their parents, so in a lot of ways this is personal for me. And let me tell you something else—what they learn out on that field? About being part of a team, of working together to achieve a goal? Totally new concept, for some of 'em. And one they'll use for the rest of their lives. Believe it or not, football's about a lot more than throwing around a funny-shaped ball. For these kids, football's not only their life. It's their *lifeline*. To something better. Something—" he lifted a hand, let it fall back to the desk "—more."

Definitely not your average jock, Claire thought. His obvious passion—for the kids even more than the sport, she was guessing—stirred something deep inside her. Compassion, maybe? Because obviously this *was* very personal for him. And not only because of his long-standing relationship with the community, but because the game was as much a lifeline for him as for them.

"I get what you're saying—"

"Really?"

She smiled. "Yes, really. But they still need to know how to write a five-paragraph essay. Especially the ones who do go on to college."

"Agreed. I'm not against the policy, per se. But I don't want them to lose the one thing that's making a positive difference in their lives."

"It's about balance, absolutely. So let's get them help." The passing bell rang. Claire stood, gathering her purse. And her now-cold coffee. "And I'll work with them, too. The unit on *Macbeth* is coming up," she said, and Ethan made a face. "Hey, I'm an actress. If I can't bring the thing to life, who can?"

"You ever tried teaching it to a bunch of high schoolers?"

"Oh, I think I'm up for the challenge." At his if-you-say-so smirk, she added, "It'll be good, I promise. Because you're not the only one who gets off on seeing them accomplish something they didn't think they could."

Ethan studied her for a moment as, outside the door, kids shuffled and shouted their way to second period. "That why you became a teacher?"

She thought for a moment. "To be honest, my goals when I went for my certification weren't nearly that altruistic. I needed a job, I liked kids and I thought teaching was something I could do until... Well. Not getting into that right now. So no, that's not why I became a teacher. But it's why I'm *glad* I did."

"Yeah. I know what you mean," he said as he stood, and somehow she got snagged in his gaze, which felt an awful lot like that memorable college performance of *A Midsummer Night's Dream* when she'd backed off the stage, got hung up on a fake tree stump and landed flat on her butt.

"Your guys won't lose their spots," she said. "Not if I can help it."

Then she booked it out of there before anything even remotely inappropriate could take root in her thoughts.

Chapter Four

"Roland? Zack? Could you stay for a couple minutes?"

Both boys were nearly through the door, making the other kids knock into them as they made their own escapes.

"We gotta get to our next class, Miss Jacobs," Roland said, dozens of meticulously crafted braids quivering around his high, toffee-colored cheekbones. "Mr. Avilla, he gets real mad if we're late."

"I've already spoken to Mr. Avilla, so you're golden. And this won't take long."

"But your next class—"

"Sophomores. Assembly." Claire indicated the desks in front of her. "So sit."

The two boys exchanged glances but trudged back to drop into their respective chairs, each one more slouched than the next. Claire, however, remained standing, scrounging for whatever psychological advantage she could get.

"I suppose you both know your grades in this class are putting your places on the team at risk."

"Yeah." Zach sighed, shoving a hand through his shaggy blond hair. "The counselor told us—"

"It's not right, man," Roland said, shaking his head. "It's only one class, it's not like we're totally failing or anything—"

Claire held up a hand, cutting him off. "Not here to argue about school policy. Which you both knew when you signed up for this gig. So. Any thoughts on how to solve the problem?"

Roland gave her the same smile Claire had noticed him using to his definite advantage on the girls. "You curve our grades? Hey!" he said when Zach smacked his arm. "What the heck—?"

"You stupid, or what? Are you even *looking* at her face, dude? Besides, if she was gonna do that, she would've done it already. Right, Miss Jacobs?"

"Since that was never even a remote possibility, Mr. Baker, your question is moot."

"Huh?"

"*M-o-o-t.* Look it up. In any case, I promised Coach Nolan I'd do everything in my power to help you pass. But you guys have to do your part, too. Which means you actually have to read the material—"

"It's *hard,* Miss Jacobs," Roland whined. "Nobody talks like that anymore—"

"Yeah," Zach put in. "I mean, that's supposed to be English?"

"As opposed to text-speak? Yes, it is. Although if you'd bothered to glance past the first page, you'd see there are footnotes on every page explaining the references *most* twenty-first-century American teenagers wouldn't get. No, it's not easy. But think how proud you'll be once you've conquered this beast. So here's the plan. First, I'm pairing you up with tutors—"

They both groaned.

"Zach, you've got Aimee Hernandez, and Roland…I thought Libby Altman would be a good fit for you."

The boys' mouths sagged open in comical unison. And no wonder. Both girls were not only knockouts and smart as whips, but probably the only two people—other than Claire—in the entire school totally immune to the football bug. As well as the boys who played it.

Roland found his voice first. "You serious, Miss Jacobs? Aimee and Libby?"

"I am."

Zach frowned. "And the girls know about this?"

"They do. And they're both looking forward to working with you." One of them, anyway. Poor Aimee nearly wet her pants at the prospect of sharing breathing space with the boy she'd been obviously sighing over since middle school. Took a little more convincing to get Libby on board, but Roland didn't need to know that. "And second…"

Claire reached behind her for a notepad, writing her cell phone number on two slips of paper, which she handed to the boys. "If you're still unclear about any of it, call me. Anytime. I'm up until at least eleven."

Zach peered up from underneath his shaggy bangs. "For real? Anytime?"

She smiled. "I may not 'get' football, although Coach Noble set me straight on how much it means to you guys. But he and I agreed it's about balance. And thinking past *now.* You won't be able to play football forever, but you will be able to use this," she said, tapping her head. "*If* it's properly trained. So…think of me as your *brain's* coach."

The boys looked at each other, then shrugged. Again, in unison.

"Yeah, guess that makes sense," Roland said.

"Good. Then we're done here. And I fully expect you two to rock the test next week."

That got dual sighs, along with a pair of resigned smiles as they hauled themselves upright. "Thanks," Zach said as he ambled out the door, but Roland hung back, just inside the classroom.

"You honestly think we're smart enough to do this?"

"Hey. I saw those plays or whatever they were on Coach Noble's blackboard. I've seen less-intimidating algebra problems. If you guys can understand those, you can understand Shakespeare."

That got a snort, followed by a slightly perplexed frown. "How come you care so much? About me and Zach, I mean. Whether we do good or not."

"I guess…because the teachers that made the biggest impression on me were the ones that made me grow, made me dig deeper and try harder. Made me feel better about myself."

"Like, more confident and stuff?"

"Exactly. So I want all my students to do *well*." She smiled. "Not *good*—"

"Like Coach Noble, huh?"

"Pardon?"

"Don't get me wrong, there's a lot of good teachers here. But it's like…most of the time, they give up on kids like me and Zach. If we get what they're talking about, fine. If we don't…" He shrugged. "Not their problem. And they *really* don't give a crap about us outside the classroom. Sure, I get it, it's not like we're their kids, they're not responsible for us. But Coach Noble… He does care. Like he did about my older brother, when he went here. Like he cares about all of us players."

He slugged his hands into his team jacket. "DeVon, he got in some trouble his sophomore year. Coach Noble, when he found out? He came to our house so he and my parents could figure out how to get DeVon's head back on straight, so he could stay on the JV team. 'Cause that's the kind of dude he is. You screw up, though, he will definitely let you know he's not happy. Coach don't take crap off of nobody. And, yeah, I know that's not correct English, it's just how I talk. Street, you know?"

Claire chuckled. "Trust me, it was the same when I went here. As long as you know the difference, it's okay. Since ain't nobody gonna give you a real job if you talk like that, yo."

He laughed. "And that sounds totally whack coming out of a white lady's mouth. But what I'm trying to say is, you going out of your way like you're doing? It reminds me of Coach."

"Is that a good thing?"

"Hell, *yeah,*" the kid said with a swat of his hand, then started toward the door.

"Roland?"

He angled back. "Yeah?"

"Your brother—what happened with him?"

His grin lit up the whole room. "Got himself a scholarship to Rutgers. Made dean's list two years running. And yeah, I know what you're gonna say—if he's that smart, I've got no excuse."

"That would definitely be my take on it, yep—"

"One more thing, though."

"And what's that?"

"I take it you don't go to the games."

"Oh, I did when I went here, back in the dark ages. But recently..." She shook her head. "No, to be honest."

"Then...if we do this for you, then you gotta come see us play. I mean, that's only fair, right?"

A smile tugged at her mouth. "I promise, I will come see you guys play. Because you're right, that is only fair. *But,*" she said when another grin flashed, "you are not doing this for me. You're doing it for yourselves. *Capiche?*"

"Whatever you say, teacher lady," he said with another grin before ambling out of the room.

Which somehow felt a lot brighter than it had ten minutes before.

Awesome.

By the time rehearsal was over and she'd forced herself to go grocery shopping—since unfortunately she was not on the food fairy's route—Claire was so tired she could barely manage a smile for her landlord when she got out of her car. Although Virgil Kane hadn't performed in years, he'd once been a staple in Maple River's community theater, so he was beyond thrilled to have a fellow thespian living upstairs. Now, bundled up like a steamship passenger crossing the North Atlantic, the little man was wedged into an old Kennedy rocker on his porch. Rain, shine or freezing weather, come six in the evening Virgil was at his post, although what he expected to see in the pitch dark, Claire had no idea. But routine kept him sane, he'd told her, especially after losing his partner of nearly five decades the spring before. And the cold, he insisted, kept him from becoming a wimp.

"Hey, Virgil," she said, setting down the bags on the top step and rummaging around in them until she found the package of cream cheese–frosted cinnamon rolls. "Got something for you while I was at the store."

"Oh, now, honey," he said, the barest breath of Southern caressing his words, "you didn't have to do that—"

"Hush, they were on sale. And I know how much you love them."

"You are such a sweet girl, honestly," he said, taking the plastic container from her. "What do I owe you?"

"Please, they were two bucks. But you might want to zap them in the microwave for a few seconds, soften 'em up a little."

"Gotcha," he said, gently setting the package on his lap, then adjusting a slightly ratty cashmere scarf around his jowls. "Oh! I talked to Gary today, he said he's directing the Little Theater's *Streetcar* in April and I immediately thought of you. Because, honey, you were *born* to play Stella."

Claire sucked in a tiny breath. *A Streetcar Named Desire?* Hell, she'd kill for a role in the iconic Tennessee Williams play.

"When are auditions?"

"After Christmas." Virgil smiled. "Shall I tell him you're interested?"

"Absolutely. Although we'll be doing the big spring musical then—*In the Heights,* although I haven't told the kids yet—so I can't jeopardize that."

"No, no, of course not…"

But as she let herself into her apartment—where the cat looked up from the sofa and yawned, clearly perturbed at having his nap interrupted—she was actually goose bumpy. Not that she'd necessarily get the part, but—

Her cell rang. She hauled it out of her purse. Local, but unfamiliar. Frowning, she cautiously answered. "Hello…?"

"You told the guys they could call you anytime?"

Ethan. In a low, rumbly, slightly pissed voice that made her goose bumpy all over again.

As well as a little pissed herself, frankly. Righteous male incredulity tended to have that effect on her. But as weary as she was, she sank onto the sofa beside the cat, who hauled himself out of his nice, warm, kittified corner to drape his purring self across her lap. Whatever Ethan Noble had to say, she was ready.

"I did," she said. *Bring it on, buster.*

Ethan's first thought, when Roland and Zach told him at practice about their meeting with Claire, was that the woman had lost her mind, giving her private number to kids she barely knew. But before he could say as much, she said, "And how, exactly, did *you* get my number?"

From the kitchen, he heard the sounds of the twins' bickering, Juliette's lame attempts to shush them, Bella's screeches about God knew what. Barney wedged his nose through the cracked-open door to what had at one time been Merri's office, clearly seeking refuge. "It's on file. Not like it's any secret."

"Oh. Right—"

"For the staff. Not for students. Seriously, what's up with getting that personal?"

"Says the guy who apparently staged a very *personal* intervention a few years back to save DeVon White's butt."

Crap. "Roland told you that?"

"He did… Omigosh—what was that?"

The crash was loud enough to make Ethan's head vibrate. But loud like a pot hitting the wood floor, not the ominous shattering of glass. "The kids are in the kitchen. Gravity happens. And DeVon saved his own butt. All I did was…" He paused.

"Light a fire under it?"

The dog stood on his hind legs to paw Ethan's lap, grinning blissfully when Ethan scratched his head. "Something like that, yeah. But that was different. Their dad's younger brother and I were on the team together, we hung out at each other's houses. So we already had a history. You don't know these boys from squat—"

"I somehow doubt they're gonna stalk me, Ethan. And my ex used to sigh like that, jeebus."

"I'm beginning to see why. And that's not the point—"

"I'm not an idiot, Ethan, it's not like I invited them home. And anyway, you want them to stay on the team, I want them to pass my class. And maybe, as a side benefit, to realize their heads are useful for something besides filling out a football helmet. I'd call that a win-win, wouldn't you?"

Ethan rubbed the space between his brows. What clearly he—or anybody else, he suspected—wouldn't win was an argument with this woman. Except then something occurred to him. "Nobody's ever gone out of their way like that for them before."

"Other than you, you mean?"

"That's different."

"How?"

"Because my job depends on my performance. Meaning it depends on my team's performance. So I have… Whaddyacallit. Incentive. To, you know, stay employed. So my own kids don't starve."

Her laugh startled him. "And you are so full of it. You think I don't hear how those boys talk about you? See how they look up to you? Because they know you care about them. As *people,* not only players. So don't give me this saving-my-job crap, 'cause I'm not buying it."

Something fisted in his chest. A memory, most likely. Of the last person who'd championed him like that. Not that his family didn't, of course. Always had. But this…

"Feisty little thing, aren't you?"

"Not so little," she muttered. "But…yeah. Because I want the best for these kids, too. All of them." He heard her take a breath. "My parents… They may not have always understood me, but they were still one hundred percent behind whatever I wanted to do. Every kid deserves that. Right?"

The dog got down, clicked out of the room. Ethan leaned back in the padded rolling chair, idly looking at the bulletin board smothered with Merri's handwritten to-do lists and schedules and what-all he'd never bothered to take down. And, in front of the board, a dozen boxes packed up and ready to ship from Jules's little eBay business. He wasn't stupid; he could hear subtext as well as the next person. He could also choose to ignore it. "So this really isn't only a job for you?"

"I told you it wasn't. Oh, my gosh...if I'd only wanted 'a job,' I could think of a dozen things easier than teaching. Like becoming one of those dudes who swallows knives."

"Or trying to make it as an actress?"

A moment passed before she said, "I'm still an actress, Ethan. Just not one pounding the streets of New York, begging for scraps from any producer or director who'll give me ten seconds of his or her time—"

The boys burst into the office, demanding Ethan immediately arbitrate a heated disagreement about who chose the next video game to play. Underneath a galaxy of freckles nearly the same color as his hair, pink splotches bloomed across Finn's cheeks.

"You got to pick last time, it's not fair!"

"I did not! You did!" Harry glowered, his perpetually tousled dark blond hair even spikier than usual. "And Mario Kart's for little kids—"

"It is not! Is it, Dad?"

"Is, too—!"

"Guys!" Ethan pointed to his phone. "Trying to have a conversation here."

"But—"

"We'll settle this later. And it's almost dinnertime, so go wash up." He waited until, both grumbling, they slogged out of the room before saying to Claire, "Sorry. You were saying—?"

"That happen a lot?"

"What? The fighting or the interrupting?"

"Whichever."

"Yes to both." Leaning forward with his elbows on the desk, Ethan released a tired chuckle. "To be honest, I haven't had an uninterrupted phone call at home since...

In a long time. Or a meal or night's sleep either, come to think of it."

"Wow."

"What can I say, it comes with the territory. But you know, one day they'll all be gone and…the silence will probably drive me insane. But where were we?" he said, sitting up again.

"Um, you're obviously busy—"

"The kids will all still be here, trust me. Unless I'm keeping you…?"

"No, no…not at all."

"Then you were saying something about…giving up on New York?"

She paused, then said, "Not so sure I gave up on New York as I came to my senses, maybe? Which I wouldn't have done if circumstances hadn't brought me back here. Gave me some space to look more objectively at my life. Because sometimes I think we keep doing things out of habit instead of rethinking whether or not we're still moving in the right direction. Whether we're still *moving* at all. And after my mother died I realized whatever I did next was entirely up to me. That my options were pretty wide-open, actually."

Then she chuckled. "Well, within reason. It's probably a pretty safe bet I'll never be a concert pianist. But I did, and do, have a lot more choices than I might've thought at one time. And right now, teaching… It really is filling something in me I didn't even know was empty—"

"Daddy?" Bella burst through the door, wearing a hoodie, a sparkly headband and a tutu. "Miss Louise says you have to watch me practice!"

"After dinner, sweetie, okay?"

"Promise?"

"I promise," he said, his chest tightening when she ran over to give him a hug, then dashed out again. *"Anyway,"* he said over Claire's chuckle. "Right now? Meaning your move back here isn't permanent?"

She snorted. "I think I've got a few minutes before I start thinking in terms of *this is it.* So who knows? Maybe I'll try New York again, find a new agent, start over. Or go out to the West Coast, see what's up out there. In the meantime, I'm happy with things as they are."

"So...no regrets?"

"About not taking Broadway by storm, you mean? It was a shot, Ethan. And I wouldn't trade the experience for anything." She paused. "No matter how many times I felt chewed up and spit out again."

"Why?" he asked, thinking about Juliette, her wide-eyed enthusiasm, her innocence, and his chest cramped. "Why would you choose to put yourself through that?"

Claire was quiet for a long moment before she said, "The same reason you went into the military, I imagine."

Ethan bristled. "Hardly the same thing."

"And yet, oddly—" he could hear the smile in her voice "—we both use the term *theater* to describe where we do our jobs."

"Okay, that's really pushing it—"

"And considering the work the USO has done for decades to boost soldiers' morale? To make them remember there's something worth fighting *for?* I don't mean to imply our choices are, or were, equal, only that they're equally valid."

"I'm not sure—"

"I mean, when I look into those kids' eyes in my classes, I think, I've got something to share with them, something *real,* something that goes way beyond how to write an essay or analyze *Of Mice and Men.* Because when I see that painfully shy kid shuck off his or her fear—of being criticized, of feeling vulnerable—and take command of the stage, or even the front of the classroom, there's no better feeling in the world—"

Now it was Jules, her face flushed, her top splotched with various food stains. "Dinner's ready!"

"Be right there," he answered. Then, to Claire, "*Now* I have go, but…okay. I'll admit, you make some good points."

Her laugh was low. One might almost say…seductive. "Yeah?"

"Yeah. And if they need a coach for the debate team? You would totally rock it."

She chuckled again. "So. Still have issues about my giving my number to the guys?"

"Yes. But I get why you did it. And…thanks."

"No problem. Oh, and I promised Roland I'd come to a game. See for myself what the fuss is all about. From a grown-up perspective, I mean. So you tell those two goofballs I expect them to play their asses off on Friday," she said, then hung up as Ethan met his oldest daughter's very curious gaze. Stanching his smile, he pawed through the mail his mother-in-law had left on the desk earlier. Mostly junk, except for the electric bill, which he ripped open, trying not to wince. Old houses had charm, but they also had zilch energy efficiency—

"Who was that?"

"Miss Jacobs," Ethan said as he stiffly got to his feet, lightly bopping the top of his firstborn's head with the mail destined for the recycle bin. "School stuff. So what's for dinner? It smells great…."

But as he followed his chatterbox firstborn back to the kitchen, he realized that, for those few minutes while he'd chatted with Claire Jacobs? He'd felt…almost good. And you know what? Sometimes, life was all about the moment. Especially when that was all it was, or ever would be.

* * *

Claire peeled the cat off her lap to finally put her groceries away, the apartment's silence enveloping her like a hug. After a day of yammering kids and brain-jarring bells, the peace of her own space was a balm to her soul. Truly. Tossing her salad stuff in the fridge, she thought of how often Ethan's kids had interrupted him, what he'd said about never getting a full night's sleep, of the constant noise and drama he lived with, day in and day out, and she smiled. Because she did not envy him one bit, no, she didn't.

Although—she dug a microwave dinner out of her freezer, kneed shut the bottom drawer—he did seem to have it all in hand, didn't he? Sure, he sounded a little tired—what parent didn't?—but she heard patience and humor and love in his voice. So much love...

She forked the plastic overwrap, shoved the tray into the microwave and her eyes stung. What the frack?

Claire looked from her tidy little kitchen to her tidy little living room, silent except for the heat humming through the vents, the microwave's whirring. Wally's purr, as he rubbed against her legs, begging. This was the life she'd chosen, a life where no one touched the TV remote except her, where if she wanted to have popcorn for dinner, she could. A life where she didn't have to clean up after anyone else or fight for the bedclothes or argue about whether or not to leave the window open.

The microwave's beep pierced her skull. She wrenched open the door, swearing when she pulled out the steaming-hot dinner and plunked it on a plastic plate. Through the closed window, she heard muffled laughter. A couple passing by, she saw when she glanced out. Arm in arm, her head against his shoulder. And she saw their future, a wedding and babies, of teenagers learning to drive and graduations and more weddings and grandbabies—

"Jeez, what is *wrong* with you?" Claire muttered as she snatched her dinner off the counter and marched the whole ten feet to her sofa, where she curled up and grabbed the remote to watch something mindless and silly and borderline appalling in its mediocrity, because she *could*.

And because anything was better than the silence.

Chapter Five

"Miss Jacobs!"

Wearing everything she owned and still about to freeze her tushie off, Claire turned in the deafening crowd surging toward the stadium entrance to see Rosie waving over her head as if she were trying to signal a ship from the shore of a deserted island. Eventually Claire thumped and bumped her way through the bodies to Juliette's grinning friend, her earmuffs barely visible in her thick, windblown hair.

"At first I wasn't sure it was you. Because, you know, I've never seen you at a game before." Her smile somehow grew brighter. "You here with anybody? 'Cause you could totally sit with us, if you want."

"Actually, I'm not." And she'd so not been looking forward to freezing to death all by her lonesome. Not that she didn't know anyone else, obviously—she was guessing at least ninety percent of the school was there—but it was clear they'd all come in groups. "So I'd love to sit with your family—"

"Oh, Dad works nights so Mom has to stay home with the younger ones. I meant with Juliette and them. Come on," she said, tugging Claire through the crowd. "Jules just texted that they're already here."

Since declining would be beyond rude, Claire meekly followed, breathing in a lungful of cold, crisp, popcorn-and-nachos-scented air when they emerged from the cement stairwell into the bleachers. Definitely not what she'd expected, let alone planned, for the evening, but she was instantly caught up in the spectacle of it all—the bright lights haloing against the almost black sky, the mouth-watering scent of junk food, the thrum of anticipation vibrating from the stands as she and Rosie threaded their way through heavy coats and blanketed knees to get to the others.

"Hey, guys, look who I found!"

Juliette looked around, her pretty face registering simultaneous surprise and delight when she spotted Claire. Squealing, the teen jumped up to give her a hug, then made her brothers scootch down to make room. The boys glanced up, gave her shy smiles, then returned to whatever they were playing on their phones. Phones! At twelve! In her day, she thought, then caught herself. Because *this* was her day—or night, whatever—and this was going to be fun, dammit. Then she realized Juliette was introducing her to an older man on the other side of her very bundled up baby sister.

"My grandfather on my dad's side," she shouted, and the tall man unfolded himself from his seat to reach across Bella and shake Claire's gloved hand.

"Preston Noble," he yelled.

"Claire Jacobs. One of the girls' teachers."

Chuckling, the elder Noble sat back down, still leaning toward her. "I've heard a lot about you. You've made quite an impression."

"A good one, I hope."

Even in the semidarkness, she could see a twinkle in the man's almost silver eyes. "Oh, very good."

A roar went up from the other side of the stadium as the visiting team was announced and their players ran out onto the field. "We'll chat later," Ethan's father said with a short salute, then pulled his little granddaughter onto his lap.

"Okay," Juliette said, having to practically sit in Claire's lap to be heard. "This is a play-off game—if Hoover wins tonight, we'll go on to the regional championship, which is played after Thanksgiving."

"So what's the Thanksgiving game?"

"Against Edison High," Rosie yelled in her other ear. "Hoover's rival." She shoved a handful of popcorn into her mouth. "It's this traditional thing that's been going on for decades."

"More for bragging rights than anything else," Preston Noble put in from several feet away. "Which doesn't mean it's not taken very seriously," he said, and both girls nodded in agreement. Then he held up a thermos. "You warm enough, Miss Jacobs? I come prepared—hot chocolate or coffee. Name your poison."

A shudder picked that moment to streak up her back with such violence she nearly fell off the bleacher. "Coffee would be terrific, thanks. And black's fine."

Nodding, Ethan's dad poured out the steaming brew into a foam cup and handed it over.

"Bless you," she said, and he gave her another salute.

"PopPop was a colonel," Juliette whispered. "In the air force. So that's what everybody calls him. The Colonel."

"Good to know," Claire said, and took that first, wonderful sip, and her insides sang hallelujah. Then another roar—five times louder—went up as Hoover High's finest poured onto the field.

"You realize you guys will have to explain this to me."

"We can do that," both girls said, and between that, and the coffee, and the crowd's boundless energy, she decided, *Y'know, this could be fun after all.*

At least she was hoping.

There was nothing like the energy pulsing through a locker room after a win, Ethan thought as he passed through the throng of bellowing, butt-slapping, high-fiving young men whose chops he'd been busting since August. One game closer to the championship. One game closer to several of his players being offered college scholarships, to further cementing his own career, maybe getting himself a raise for next year. Another change of plans he'd never seen coming, God knew. But seeing the joy on the guys' faces, feeling the pride surging through him—in both them and himself... Right now, there was nothing better and nowhere he'd rather be.

Once the locker room cleared, he headed out, the cold air a welcome relief from the hot, smelly stadium underbelly. Maybe it was the adrenaline rush, maybe it was the general atmosphere, but his knee wasn't even bothering him as he walked around to meet up with the others, then go on to their favorite place for dinner like they always did after an early game.

"Daddy! Daddy!" Bella called out, running up with outstretched arms. "PopPop said we won!"

"We sure did, sugarplum," Ethan said, kissing his baby on her cold cheek and making her giggle. A moment later the twins were in his face as well, both talking at once about their favorite moments:

"Defense totally rocked tonight, didn't it, Dad?" Finn asked, bouncing as they walked back toward the others.

"They sure did—" Wait...who was that with them?

Harry stumbled over his suddenly size-twelve feet, knocking against Ethan's arm. Ethan caught the boy before he fell flat on his face even as the kid said, "And then White made that touchdown with five seconds left on the clock! Holy cow!"

Holy cow was right, Ethan thought as he got close enough to see Claire. Clutching her coat collar as if she was about to freeze right on the spot, she grinned at him, her eyes bright. Although from what, he couldn't say.

"Look who Rosie found before the game!" Jules said, her breath puffing around her face. "So she sat with us and we taught her stuff."

"Relating to the game, I hope," Ethan said, and his oldest girl rolled her eyes.

"Da-ad, jeez…"

"And what did you think?" Ethan asked Claire, immediately sucked into her glittering brown gaze.

"I thought it was, to use a common parlance, awesome," she said with a light laugh even as she shivered. "G-granted, I still had no clue what was going on half the time, but I haven't had that much fun in ages. Seriously, it was like being at a rock concert." Ethan pushed a breath through his lips, and she grinned. "And Roland kicked serious *butt*."

"She said a bad word, Daddy," Bella said, and Claire clamped her hand over her mouth.

"I'm so sorry, sweetie," she said, lowering it. "I won't say it again, I promise."

"That's okay," Bella said with a serious nod, and Ethan nearly choked with trying to keep a straight face. "Since it's not one of the *really* bad ones."

With that, the laugh burst out anyway, mingling with Claire's under a starry sky in an empty high school parking lot, and Bella laughed, too, in his ear, even though she obviously had no idea what was so funny. Then Ethan glanced past Claire to see Juliette's wide eyes, his father giving him a thumbs-up. Brother.

"Your dad invited me to come with you guys to Murphy's," Claire said. "Hope that's okay?"

"Of course." Because he felt too damn good to let a little thing like a busybody father and a cute-as-hell brunette with sparkling brown eyes and a laugh that promised things she probably had no idea she was promising ruin the high he was riding. Something he didn't get too often these days, not like this—another one of those *moments*—and like hell was he gonna let it go just yet.

Even if Claire Jacobs and her sparkling eyes were part of that high.

Claire hadn't been inside Murphy's in... Hell. A million years. But as they all smushed inside the packed restaurant, it all came roaring back—the come-to-mama aroma of onion rings and charred beef, the dark-paneled walls choked with signed senior portraits dating back to the seventies, when the place first opened. The noise, easily rivaling that of a pair of subway trains passing each other through a tiled tunnel. The warmth.

Speaking of which... Holding his little girl again, Ethan was standing close enough to Claire that his arm pressed into her shoulder. Solid. Sturdy. Nice.

Sigh.

Oh, she was here entirely of her own volition. She'd driven herself to the game, and she could have easily refused the Colonel's invitation...despite Juliette's and Rosie's earnest pleas for her to accept. But you know what? One, she was absolutely starving, the kind of hunger that nothing short of some hideously caloric burger-and-fries combo was going to sate. And two, so sue her, despite being unable to feel her toes at times, she'd had a blast. And she wasn't ready for it to be over yet. Even if that meant being squished next to Ethan Noble for a minute or two or six while they waited for a table.

Sigh, redux.

Knowing she was close to endangering her hormones' immortal souls, she glanced up. Bella had nestled herself good and tight against her daddy's chest to lay her head on his shoulder, facing Claire, from which vantage point she gave Claire a sweet "life is good, huh?" smile. Claire smiled back and the little girl grinned more broadly and, okay, there might've been some heart tugging going on. And not only because the kid was so fricking cute, but because Claire remembered her own dad holding her like that. And how safe she'd felt in his arms. Safe, and loved.

"Sorry," Ethan said over his baby's head. "It's always nuts here after a game."

"I remember," Claire said, having to seriously invade his space so he could hear her. And hence, nearly passing out from how terrific he smelled. "In fact, my friends and I usually avoided Friday nights at all costs. But that was then. This is now. And now is good."

Ethan gave her a funny look, then nodded. "You're right. Now—this moment—*is* good. So—"

"Noble! Party of eight! This way, please!"

The harried little hostess hustled them over to their table—two tables, actually, pushed together—smack in the middle of everything. The Colonel anchored one end, Ethan the other, and in the mad scramble to get seated Claire found herself between one of the twins and the Colonel and across from the girls. Where, you know, she was safe from penetrating gazes and such from handsome widowers. As were her hormones.

Whew, close.

While they waited for their food, the Colonel grilled her about her New York days, allowing Claire to dredge up some almost forgotten and borderline hair-raising stories. Rosie looked horrified, the Colonel amused and Juliette enthralled, leaning forward with her chin in her hands.

"I cannot *wait*," she finally said when two servers arrived to set sizzling platters of greasy yumminess in front of them. "It must be so boring being back here."

"Not at all," Claire said, chomping an onion ring large enough to encircle Saturn. "A lot quieter, maybe." Grinning, she waved the ring to indicate their surroundings. "Most of the time, anyway. But there is nothing even remotely boring about working with you guys. And anyway, I've always felt it's my choice whether to be bored or not. There's always something to do, even if it's only listening to music. Or reading," she said with a pointed look at the girls, who both rolled their eyes.

"What about being lonely?" Juliette asked, stuffing a fry in her mouth.

Claire didn't miss a beat, even if her heart did. "Same thing. Because honestly, if you enjoy your own company, how can you be lonely? Also, as you get older, you'll discover that solitude can be a very precious thing."

Rosie laughed. "Clearly you haven't met my family. But it's all good, since I probably wouldn't know what to do with myself if I were ever really alone."

"Yeah. Same here," Juliette said, sighing, and Claire chuckled even as she caught the Colonel's pensive expression. For a moment she considered laying a hand on his wrist to let him know she understood what he was feeling. She remembered how hard the holidays had been on her mother after her dad's passing. On her, too, of course, but not the same way. After all, Claire's future still beckoned, full of promise. Not like—as her mother had said often enough—a big, dark void.

Then her attention drifted down the table to Ethan, as he calmly listened to the boys still going on about the game while trying to get Bella to eat at least one bite of the broccoli he'd ordered with her chicken tenders. Silly man, she thought, smiling, as his eyes lifted to hers, and he smiled back. But she could tell the earlier euphoria was already fading, swallowed up in reality.

It's okay, Claire mouthed, although she had no idea what had possessed to say such a thing at all, let alone to him. Although with any luck he'd think she meant the broccoli debacle rather than anything deeper. And far more personal.

Looking away, she took another bite of the most bodacious burger in Jersey, wiping her chin as she glanced around at the restaurant's interior, familiar and strange all at once. Like Maple River itself had felt for weeks after she'd returned. Sure, there were changes out on the highway—new stores, new places to eat—but here, in the town's heart, so much was both eerily and comfortingly the same. Home, she thought with a bittersweet pang.

"They still put up those tacky tinsel Christmas decorations?" she asked the table at large.

"You mean the ones from when we were in school?" Ethan said, taking a napkin to Bella's greasy hands as the child pronounced herself done. Chicken 3, broccoli 0. "Yep. Wouldn't be Christmas otherwise—"

"Dad?" Juliette said. "I forgot to tell you—I'm helping Kelly do Thanksgiving dinner over at PopPop's, so I won't be able to watch the other kids at the game."

"Oh. Well, I guess we'll work something out. Maybe they could go to Pop's house early."

The boys both looked horror-struck.

"And miss the game?"

"No way!"

"Then let me see if either of your uncles are going—"

"I can take them," Claire said, and a half-dozen heads swiveled in her direction. "If you can't get anyone else, I mean."

"You sure?"

"You sound skeptical."

Ethan nodded sideways at the boys, currently seeing which one could stuff the most fries in his mouth. Claire sighed. Right. But…

"I think I can manage. Besides, it's not like I'm doing anything else that day."

"At *all?*" Juliette asked.

Claire laughed. "We didn't do much when I was growing up. With three people, there's no sense cooking a turkey, and Mom wasn't much of a cook, anyway. So it's never been a big deal for me."

"But what do you *do?*"

She shrugged. "Watch the Macy's parade in my jammies. That dog show that comes on afterward. *It's a Wonderful Life.*" She grinned. "Then I eat an entire pumpkin pie by myself. Which is glorious, believe me. But," she said, turning to Ethan, "I can easily DVR the parade and the dog show and watch them later, so I could certainly take the boys to the game—"

"And then you're coming for dinner," the Colonel said. "Because nobody should be alone on Thanksgiving. You hear me?"

"Yeah, what he said," Juliette put in, practically quivering with excitement. "Then you can meet everybody else, too. Well, mostly, I think my aunt Sabrina is going to her fiancé's out on the island. But it'll be so much fun! Please say yes. *Please?*"

Oh, dear. Claire glanced down the table at Ethan, who was so busy dealing with Bella about something that Claire wondered if he'd even heard his father's invitation. So what his reaction to said invitation might be, she had no clue. Hers, however…

How to explain that, that day alone? Eating pie all by herself? It was her sanctuary. Or had been, for years. She'd rarely even accepted friends' invitations when she'd been in New York, that Great Gathering of Strays that happened every year, turning colleagues and strangers into family, even if for only one day. Oddly, not Claire's thing. So now, faced with the prospect of, once again, pretending to be part of something she wasn't, making small talk with people she didn't know… Ack.

Except then Ethan said, "Dad's right. Nobody should be alone on Thanksgiving."

Her heart pounding, Claire lifted her eyes to see him watching her, his steady gaze damn close to…a challenge? What the hell? Then she turned again to catch the brightness in Juliette's eyes, hope in the Colonel's. Although she knew what lay behind the girl's excitement—alas— she had no idea why her presence was so important to her grandfather. But it clearly was. And she couldn't find it in herself to disappoint the older man. Or worse, come across as either rude or even weirder than she was.

"Then I'd love to come," she said, which got a huge smile from Juliette and a sharp, approving nod from Ethan's father, as though she'd given the right answer. And from Ethan? An expression—from what she could tell anyway, when she dared another glance in his direction—she couldn't even begin to read.

Guess it was time to figure out how to set her DVR….

By the time Thanksgiving morning arrived, Claire had decided that the grease fumes at Murphy's must've gotten to her the other night. Because what else could have possibly possessed her to take responsibility for a pair of twelve-year-old boys for two hours?

However, a promise was a promise. So she girded her loins—with thermal long johns, actually—said goodbye to Wally, who twitched his tail at her from sunlit windowsill, then hied her thermalized booty to the school, where she was to collect the boys from Ethan so he could go on the bus with the team to the college stadium where the game was being played.

All three were in Ethan's office, the boys slumped in a pair of chairs against the wall, all knees and elbows as they played games on their phones. Spikes of dark blond hair seemed determined to escape from Harry's brightly patterned knit hat, complete with a fetching tassel and a pair of braided ties hanging down to his shoulders, while Finn's thin, freckled face with its high cheekbones peeked out from a fake fur–rimmed hood. Her stomach clutched again. What would they talk about? And what if they had to go to the bathroom—?

Ethan stood, his expression indicating he'd been doing some second-guessing of his own. In the grayish glow from the fluorescent lighting, he looked as though his responsibilities weighed on him like anvils. And yet, amusement still flickered in his eyes, the humor of a man trying to make the best of things.

"Happy Thanksgiving," he said, a small smile touching his lips. As though he knew full well that right now she was seriously questioning her sanity. Then she thought, *Okay, this is nuts, I can handle a couple of kids. Right?*

"You, too. Okay, guys—let's get a move on."

"Wait," Ethan said as his sons slowly roused themselves and got to their oversize feet, stretching and yawning. He pulled out his wallet, handed her a pair of bills. "The secret is to keep them fed. Early and often."

"So I noticed. But I don't need—"

"Take the money. No arguments."

"Yeesh, you're as bad as your dad," she said, and his forehead knotted for a moment before he walked over, grabbed her hand and pressed the bills into it. And yeah, things fluttered. Strike that—more like jerked to attention with a *what the hell?*

"Yes, I am. And you'll thank me later, trust me."

"Hey, Coach," one of his assistants said from the office door. "We're just waiting for you."

"Be right there." Then he turned a stern eye on his sons. "You guys listen to Miss Jacobs, you hear me? Do whatever she tells you."

"Yeah, yeah, Dad," Harry said. "We'll be good, promise."

"Promise," echoed Finn.

"Meet back here after?" he said, and Claire nodded, and then Ethan was gone and she was left alone with a pair of seventh-graders who were taller than she was, loping behind her like a pair of Great Dane puppies.

"Can we stop at McDonald's or someplace on the way there?" somebody said from the backseat after they were buckled in. "I'm starving."

"Yeah, me, too," chimed the other one, and Claire sighed.

"Sure thing," she said, thinking, *Two hours. I can do this....*

As usual, until the buzzer sounded at the end of the game—which had ended in a frustrating tie, since the overtime rules were suspended because of the holiday— Ethan had remained focused on the game, relying on a two-decades-old ability to compartmentalize his feelings. Not that he didn't occasionally wonder how Claire was getting on with the twins, but he'd refused to dwell on it. If she could handle a class of thirty hormonized juniors, she could handle a pair of twelve-year-old boys, right?

Even so, when they met up after the game he was grateful to see that she wasn't twitching *too* badly, although there was no denying the relief on her face when she caught sight of him. The same as there was no denying a brief but nearly overwhelming urge on his part to give her a hug, reassure her she'd done good. Since, after all, both boys were still with her and no one was missing a limb.

Instead, he settled for giving her a thumbs-up before sticking both hands into his jacket pockets, his chest twinging a little at her slightly frazzled smile.

"Sorry you guys didn't win," she said, and he shrugged, even as he noted the "you guys" bit. As opposed to, say, "we."

"It's okay, it happens. They both played good games, that's all. And it'll only fire up everybody even more next year."

"You weren't kidding about the food consumption," she said over the grunts and shouts of the boys' tussling with each other behind her. Merri had always said it was because they'd spent the first nine months of their lives entwined in the womb that they couldn't seem to stay away from each other for longer than thirty seconds, although Ethan suspected that was due more to their being boys than anything else. "Where on earth do they put it all?"

"We've long suspected they have extra stomachs. Like cows. So you survived, I see."

"I did. Although I may need a nap before the day's out." Harry poked Finn, and they were off, zooming around the nearly empty parking lot. Ethan heard Claire chuckle. "They're like a pair of cheetahs, aren't they?"

"Not as graceful, but yeah." His eyes narrowed. "See how Finn keeps dodging Harry? It's still too early to tell, of course, but I think the kid has real potential as a wide receiver. Because of his agility," he explained. "It's hard to catch him."

She nodded. "And Harry?"

"Not sure yet about him. He likes the game well enough, but I don't think his heart's in it. Not like his brother. Baseball, though... Now, that, he loves. So we'll see."

"And you're good with that?"

"Why wouldn't I be? Kid's gotta do what makes him happy."

"I see," she said, in that way women did when there was a lot more to say. "So. Your dad said to come around two or so, which gives me time to go back home and take that nap—"

"For real?"

She laughed. "In case you hadn't noticed, those two are major energy suckers. Don't get me wrong, they weren't any trouble—"

"You sure?"

"They're great kids, Ethan," she said, then looked back at the boys. "And they think the world of you. Omigosh, they're so proud of their dad, when you're out there on the field… It's adorable."

He huffed a laugh. "Now there's a word I haven't associated with those two since they were six months old."

Laughing a little herself, she smiled up at him again. "We had fun. Yes, honestly. But I definitely need to recharge." She made a face at what looked like a mustard stain on her jeans. "And change. I swear, I cannot be trusted around condiments."

"I apologize for my father strong-arming you about coming to dinner."

Her forehead knotted and she glanced up at him. Then, looking away, she smiled. "He is a hard man to say no to."

"You're telling me," Ethan muttered, and her eyes cut back to his. "As kids, we all quickly learned not to argue with him. It's that military training. It seeps into the blood." He smiled. "*Flexible* was not a word any of us would have ever used to describe him."

"As in strict?"

"Consistent was more like it. But it was that very consistency that saved so many kids' butts. Made them—us—feel…secure."

"Isn't that what any parent wants for his kids?"

"Well, yeah. Of course. And he set a great example. But he can also be pushy as hell. So please don't feel you *have* to go."

Their gazes tangled for a long moment before Claire said, very softly, "I don't." Then she started walking backward toward her car, the breeze tugging at her curls. "So I'll see you there—?"

"Need directions?"

"I've got the address, it's not far from my place. Bye, guys!" she yelled to the kids, who waved over at her before trooping back to Ethan, panting and grinning.

Ethan grabbed Harry around the shoulders to give him a one-armed hug as Finn shoved his hands into his parka's pockets, his goofy grin more and more reminding Ethan of the one picture he had of his birth father—

"So what'd Miss Jacobs say?" Finn asked. "About us?"

"That you were good. Why?" Ethan said when the boys exchanged a glance. "Is there something I should know?"

"Nuh-uh," Finn said, the sun glinting off his spiky red hair. "And Miss Jacobs… She's okay, too. Even if she did ask, like, a million questions so it was kinda hard to concentrate on the game. So when's dinner? I'm starving."

"Yeah, me, too," Harry said.

"I swear, I'm about to hook you two up to an IV," Ethan muttered as they started across the lot toward his car, and the boys laughed, making him smile, even as it killed him that Merri was missing all this.

Then again, it occurred to him on the drive back to his dad's, maybe she wasn't. Maybe the dead really could keep tabs on the ones left behind, what the hell did he know? But even if Merri was somehow aware of what was going on, that didn't stop Ethan's pain, did it? Not entirely.

Not enough.

Certainly not enough to risk going through that particular brand of hell again, he thought as Claire's slightly shell-shocked expression, her obvious covering for the boys' antics, invaded his thoughts, making him smile in spite of himself. She was something else, that Claire.

Much like a certain pretty blonde who hadn't been like all the others either, a girl he'd fallen so hard for that when she left, he could barely get up again. Oh, he had, of course, for their kids' sakes. And here he was, plodding along day after day, doing what needed to be done… A poster child for the walking wounded. In more ways than one, he thought as his knee briefly throbbed from the morning's exertion.

Yeah, life was plenty good already at tripping up a person when he least expected it. To let himself get caught in the trap when he could see it, plain as day…

That was just plain stupid.

Minutes later, they walked into his childhood home, smelling of roasting turkey and pumpkin pie, and nostalgia collided with longing as the twins torpedoed to the kitchen to scavenge. Before he could catch up, he heard Jules shriek at her brothers to keep their mitts off whatever it was they had in their sights. His five months' pregnant sister-in-law Kelly, however, was laughing and telling the boys they could take whatever they wanted, not to worry.

And no wonder, Ethan saw when he got there. Because save for two tiny spaces on the granite island where Jules and Kelly were working, trays and platters and serving dishes of food took up every square inch of the surface. With goody-laden paper plates, the boys took off again, trailed by a chocolate Newfoundland and a boxer mix, Ethan's brothers' dogs.

"Jeez, Kell…" Ethan plucked a couple black olives from the already decimated relish tray, popping them into his mouth before he registered the classical music playing from her iPod. He tensed—since Merri's death, he'd deliberately not listened to the music she'd loved so much. But he pulled himself together and asked, "How many people you expecting?"

The redhead grinned. "With this family? You never know. Extras happen." She frowned at the appetizers tray. "Um…Jules? You mind getting another couple cans of olives from the pantry?" After the girl left, Kelly turned to Ethan, her voice lowered. "Speaking of extras… Jules tells me her teacher is coming?"

"Yep," he said, punching his hands into his Hoover jacket. Playing it cool. "She was at the game on Friday, went out with us to Murphy's after. Pop invited her. You know how those things go."

"Oh, I do," Kelly said, deftly cutting little crescents in the crust of some sort of fruit pie before sliding it into the upper oven. "So what's she like?"

Ethan almost laughed. Honestly, what *was* it with women? "And you're asking this, why? Especially since you'll find out for yourself soon enough."

Kelly climbed onto a bar stool across from him, snitching one of the olives herself. "I'm asking because your daughter seems inordinately excited about this turn of events." She shrugged. "So I'm curious."

"She's her favorite teacher, that's all," Ethan said with a shrug of his own. "Seems to get the kids. Nice lady."

Another olive disappeared. "I see," Kelly said, as Jules plunked the cans on the counter.

"Um…if you don't need me for a while…?"

"Nope, not until one-thirty," Kelly said with a smile. "So begone with you, child." And, as a giggling Jules hightailed it out of the kitchen, Ethan felt at least some of the tension he'd been carrying around for what seemed like forever slough off his shoulders. In the past year, both his brothers had brought new aunts into the family, at least partially filling the gap in his children's lives. Sure, they'd had his sisters, who loved the kids to bits. But Sabrina had her life in Manhattan and was therefore rarely around, and Abigail was too young at twenty-three to be much of a mother figure. Kelly, however, as well as Tyler's fiancée, Laurel, provided excellent role models for his girls.

Meaning Jules would eventually realize she already had what she needed without trying to fit someone else into the family routine.

"So Jules tells me she finally caved and got a math tutor?"

"Yeah," Ethan breathed out. "Some geeky senior, I gather."

"How's that going?"

"She passed her last test, so I'm guessing okay." Ethan suddenly noticed the army of pies lined up on the counter, including no less than a half dozen pumpkin. Following his gaze, Kelly snorted.

"Yeah, I might've gotten a little carried away."

"Ya think? I mean, we all like pie, sure, but…" He frowned. "You think I could set one of the pumpkins aside for…for later?"

"Since half of 'em are gonna go home with you guys, anyway… Wait. I thought Jules said you weren't a big pumpkin pie fan?"

"It's…not for me."

Kelly gave him a curious look, then shrugged. "There's pie boxes in the pantry. Go for it."

Ethan carted off one of the fragrant, glistening pies to tuck it away, then returned to the kitchen in time to see his younger brother, Matt—with Kelly's curly-haired four-year-old daughter, Aislin, perched on his hip like a little monkey—give his still-new wife a quick kiss.

"You doing okay?" he asked, palming her growing belly, his darker Hispanic coloring a riveting contrast to Kelly's ivory complexion, and a pang of envy pierced Ethan's genuine happiness for his brother.

Kelly laughed, breaking the spell. "I'm fine. Although I think…" She yawned, then smiled. "I might go take a quick nap before the final push." She got up, then leaned over to give her little girl a noisy kiss on her cheek. "You be good for Daddy, 'kay?"

"'Kay."

After she left, Ethan sensed his brother watching him. He looked over, frowning at Matt's all-too-knowing expression. His cop look, they called it. The music changed, to some piano piece he'd always associate with Merri. Rachmaninoff, he thought. "What?" he pushed through a tight throat.

But Matt only gave Ethan's shoulder a quick squeeze before carrying his daughter out of the room, and Ethan scrubbed a hand down his face, ignoring the knot in the center of his chest, his stinging eyes.

It'll get easier, everyone had said. *Just give it time….*

Which was the biggest lie since Santa, he thought on a bitter, bitter sigh.

Chapter Six

The Colonel's house was even closer than Claire had first realized, a short walk through the very pretty neighborhood of restored Queen Annes, handsome redbrick Colonials, the occasional Craftsman duplex. It'd be dark by the time the party broke up, but after late-night treks and subway rides through at least three of New York's five boroughs, Maple River's sleepy streets held no terror.

Although the prospect awaiting her sure did. Honestly, it was like being sixteen all over again, when she had the crush *that would not die* on Brandon Hicks, who sat two rows ahead of her in U.S. History. Every time she saw him, her mouth would go dry and her heart rate would ramp to warp speed. And the one time he smiled at her—although he might've been smiling for someone behind her, she was too freaked to find out for sure—she'd nearly wet her pants. So sad.

The good news was, Claire mused as she turned onto the Colonel's block, she was much more in control of her bladder these days. Not to mention other things. Okay, so her attraction to Ethan Noble wasn't waning the *more* she got to know him, which wasn't good. At all. But since that attraction was completely illogical—if not downright stupid, especially given his obvious attempt at giving her an out if she'd decided not to show—*and* since she wasn't sixteen anymore, thank God, she could handle it. And anyway, she was here for Ethan's father. And the food.

Her heart ramming against her rib cage, she paused at the end of the brick walk leading to the lovely Victorian, glowing in the midafternoon sunshine. It was easily twice the size of Ethan's house, as was the lot it sat on. Impressive. But not, she decided, channeling Julie Andrews in *The Sound of Music* as she marched up the walk, intimidating.

That's right. Confidence, she had it.

Dogs barked when she rang the doorbell; a second later, the white paneled door swung open and Juliette let out a squeal, not even trying to keep the dogs—Claire momentarily thought one of them was a bear, good God—from joyously accosting her.

"You're really here!" The orange streaks in her hair matching her lacy cropped sweater and the patterned tights covering the vast amount of leg her short denim skirt didn't, Juliette tugged Claire through the wriggling beasts and into a shabbily graceful foyer with worn wooden floors and faded Oriental rugs, a staircase wall choked with framed photos.

"I really am." Claire shrugged off her coat, breathing in the turkey-scented steam heat as she chafed the sleeves of her favorite sweater, a handkerchief-hemmed cardi that discreetly hid the result of her penchant for cheesecake. "Did you think I wouldn't come?"

"Were you sure you would?" the girl asked bluntly, and Claire laughed, waggling her hand. The teen grinned, then nodded toward a multipeg rack on the wall. "You can hang your coat there with the rest. Then come back to the kitchen and I'll introduce you to Kelly. My new aunt," she added with a very pleased grin. Claire thought of all the fifteen-year-olds she knew who reeked of bored cynicism despite privileged, even charmed, lives. This kid *knew* from heartbreak, and yet she seemed to genuinely appreciate what she had rather than grieving what she'd lost.

"Where's everyone else?"

"Out back. Football," Juliette said with such a face Claire had to laugh. "I'm guessing you don't want to play?"

"Um, no," she said, and the girl giggled, then sobered as she—and the dogs—led Claire back to the kitchen.

"When we were little," Juliette said, "Grandma would put the turkey in the oven, then we'd all go to the game, and then we'd come back here to finish up the cooking. And then we'd eat. Like, for days. Then Grandma died, so Mom took over the turkey."

At the girl's silence, Claire looked over, her heart turning over at her expression. She laid a hand on the slender shoulder, and the teen sucked in a breath.

"It's so weird, how it just…hits. Like totally out of nowhere."

"I know, honey. Believe me."

Juliette nodded, then said on a sigh, "Anyway…for the past couple of years, PopPop's been getting the turkey already cooked from ShopRite, and Dad and I would make a few sides, but…it wasn't the same. Now, though, with Kelly and everything—she has her own catering business, she's, like, the most amazing cook ever—it already feels *so* much better. Different, sure. But at least not like everyone's faking it…. Hey, Kelly!" she said when they reached the kitchen, where a very pretty redhead was taking rolls out of the oven. "This is Miss Jacobs!"

Anyone else in the midst of the last-minute holiday-meal insanity would have been at her wit's end. At least Claire certainly would have been. But although her curls—nearly as wild as Claire's—were clearly nya-nya-nya-ing the black satin headband ostensibly keeping them in place, the woman's smile was warm.

"Welcome to the land of the loonies," Kelly said with a laugh. In the center of the island proudly gleamed a golden brown turkey the size of a small planet. "I assume I don't have to call you Miss Jacobs?"

"Oh, God, no. Claire is fine."

"Ooh, pretty name. Jules, sweetie? Check the broccoli, make sure it's *just* tender before you drain it. And the sweet-potato casserole should be about ready to come out of the other oven."

"On it!"

"Need any help?"

"Nope," Kelly said, her emerald-green Shaker sweater molded to a pooched-out tummy. "The kid and I, we've got this planned out to the second. But if you want to pitch in for cleanup...?"

"That I can do."

"Great. Then why don't you go watch the game? Since it's at least a half hour before dinner..."

Because Claire hadn't already seen more football in the past week than she'd seen in the ten years prior. But since she'd clearly only get in the way in the kitchen, she followed the shouting and laughter to the back porch overlooking a large, generously planted yard, bordered with forty-foot pines glittering in the sun. In one corner stood a weathered play set—three swings, a slide, a small fort—currently commandeered by Bella and a smaller girl, her light brown curls barely visible beneath a bright pink pom-pommed knit hat. Between the set and the deck, in still-green grass dotted with the occasional red leaf, the game was in full swing, Ethan "coaching" one team while an equally tall, darker-haired man headed up another.

Wrapping up in a throw left to languish on the porch railing, Claire settled into a sunlight-drenched rocker to watch the game. Or rather, to watch Ethan from a safe distance, where she could relish the attraction for its own sake without worrying about What It All Meant. She thought of poor Juliette, in the throes of unrequited puppy love for Scott Jenkins—yes, she'd noticed the girl's longing glances at rehearsals—and sent up a short prayer of thanks that her own teenage years were long gone, when all too often she'd felt downright *possessed* by things she didn't even fully understand. She wouldn't want to feel that out of control again for anything.

"So you're here," she heard a few feet away, yanking her out of her thoughts. Claire looked up to see the Colonel standing by the steps, his hands in his corduroy pants' pockets. The dogs followed him, collapsing by his feet with matching doggy groans.

"Wouldn't've missed it," Claire said, and the older man smiled, his blue eyes sparkling underneath close-cropped hair she now realized was more white than silver.

"How come you're not out there with everyone else?"

"Heh. I might be at the place where I'll actually watch football. But play it? No way."

The Colonel chuckled. Even so, in the daylight—and his own house—his bearing was far more daunting than it had been the other night. She thought of her own dad, who'd been smaller, thinner, bookish rather than athletic. But behind his wire-rimmed glasses, there'd always been so much love in those warm brown eyes. Same as there'd been in her mother's. And at that moment, she missed them so much she could barely breathe.

"I hope that doesn't mean I forfeit my place at the dinner

table," she said, to tease herself out of her maudlin mood as much as anything.

"Oh, I suppose not," the Colonel said. "Since you're already here."

Snuggling more deeply into the throw, Claire smiled. The smaller of the dogs roused himself to come over, his entire back end wriggling as he laid his jowly chin on her knee. Claire scratched the top of his wrinkly head, and the beast shut his eyes in obvious bliss. "This is a lovely house."

"Thanks. It's been good to us all these years. Time to let it go, though."

"Oh? Too bad."

The older man shrugged. "Don't need a place this big anymore. Five bedrooms…" His head slowly wagging, he turned to lean against a post, his arms crossed. "So Julie tells me this is your first year at Hoover?"

"It is."

"You like it?"

"I do. Not that there aren't…challenges," she said with another smile, petting the dog some more when he nosed her hand. "And I'm still feeling my way with the kids, finding that balance between not being a stick-in-the-mud but not being a pushover, either. All in all, though, it's a pretty good gig."

The Colonel looked out over the yard. "Ethan said you came back here to help your mother when she got sick."

"Yeah. She's been gone about a year now."

That cool blue gaze met hers again. "And you're still here."

"I am. At least until—"

"Something better comes along?"

Claire smiled. "Until being here no longer feels like a good fit."

Ethan's father paused, then said, "After more years of

base housing than I care to remember, I don't think it ever even occurred to Jeannie and me that we'd end up right back where we both grew up. But then a position opened up at McGuire Air Force Base, and Jeannie found this house, and..." He smiled. "So you never know what life's got in store."

"No," Claire said quietly. "You sure don't. If it's one thing life isn't, it's static."

The Colonel's lips tilted in a half smile before he resumed watching the game. "God knows, we didn't expect so many of the kids to hang around, set down their own roots here. So I guess it's not such a bad place to live...." Since he seemed to be talking to himself more than to her, Claire didn't answer. Then he asked, "You get introduced to everyone?"

"Not yet, no. I met Kelly, though, in the kitchen."

"Then let's see if I can remember all the names," the Colonel said as he lowered himself into the rocker next to hers, crossing his arms over a heavy brown cardigan Claire guessed had some serious years on it. "You know Ethan's brood, so I won't bother with them. But the other coach? That's Matt, our next oldest. He's married to Kelly. Kid in the glasses is her son by her first marriage, Cooper. And the cutie on the swing's his sister, Aislin, better known as Linnie. Now, over there..." He leaned closer, pointing. "That's Tyler, our youngest son—"

"The one who looks like trouble waiting for a place to happen?"

The Colonel chuckled. "Got that one pegged, all right. He's gonna marry Laurel—she had a baby not all that long ago, the father... Well, we don't talk about him. Anyway...the skinny little blond thing is Abby, Jeannie's and my youngest, who's living proof that God has a sense of humor. We'd been married more than twenty years, no kids of our own, and then boom. Here comes Abby." He glanced over, humor dancing in his eyes. "Your head spinning yet?"

"Ever so slightly. How on earth do you keep track of everyone? *Did* you, when you cared for all those fosters?"

"You learn to go with the flow, I guess. What you said about life not being static? Same goes for family. Even with 'normal' families, whatever that means these days, the dynamic is always in a state of flux. People are added and subtracted, babies are born and old people pass away." He got quiet. "Sometimes, not so old. But it's like Jeannie's rosebushes over there." He waved toward a couple dozen lifeless-looking bushes, barren except for the occasional fat, rust-colored rose hip. "Come spring, there's always new flowers to replace the old ones from the year before."

Hard to believe that this sentimental old man was the rod-up-his-rear disciplinarian Ethan had made him out to be. Although given what it must have been like with all those kids in the house, without at least some semblance of order things could have easily degenerated into anarchy. A mind-set that, from what she'd observed both with his kids and his players, had clearly rubbed off on Ethan. At least to some degree.

Turning this thought over in her head, Claire said, "Wasn't like that with my family, though. Me and my parents—that was it, basically."

"No other relatives? Grandparents?"

She shook her head. "They were both only children, too. And older. And their parents…" Her mouth tightened. "Dad was Jewish, Mom Italian. Catholic. Not even an issue for most people anymore, but it was for my grandparents. I did see them occasionally, but only at their houses, with that parent. So holidays were…very subdued."

"That's one thing they definitely were not around here. Or any other day, for that matter," Preston said with a soft chuckle. "I assumed, as I got older, I'd welcome the peace. I was wrong. The noise, the barely controlled chaos... I miss it. I really do."

Having nothing to say to that, Claire watched Ethan huddle with his "team," thinking how hard the day—or at least this part of it—had to be on him. Especially after what Juliette had said about her mother keeping the holiday tradition alive after Ethan's mother's passing. And yet, there he was, doing the brave-faced thing for his kids, the rest of his family...

Her heart ached.

Then he straightened from the huddle and backed away, shouting as he pumped his fist, like she'd seen him do on the field. Except now she noticed a limp she hadn't before. "Am I imagining things, or does Ethan's leg seem to be bothering him?"

A moment passed before the Colonel said, "It's his knee. He blew it out when he was over in Afghanistan. A month from coming home, too."

"Oh, no... I didn't know."

"Few people do. Doesn't stop him from functioning normally—for the most part, anyway—but it did put the kibosh on his playing professionally."

Claire looked at the older man's profile. "He was that good?"

"Better," he said after a moment. "Don't tell him I said anything, he hates talking about it. Doesn't want anybody to feel sorry for him—"

The screen door banged open, followed by Juliette tramping out onto the porch long enough to yell that dinner was ready. After some grumbling from down in the yard, everyone trooped back to the house. Claire stood so Ethan's father could formally introduce her to everyone, and she sent up yet another prayer of gratitude that her socially awkward days were long behind her. That she had absolutely nothing to fear.

Until Ethan's gaze snagged in hers, and...

Crap.

Seeing Claire and his father chatting away like they were old friends... It'd blown Ethan's concentration to hell and back. Because the man who'd raised him might be of few words—or at least, he used to be—but those words tended to be cut-to-the-quick honest. Subtle had never been the Colonel's style. Since it clearly wasn't Claire's either, heaven only knew how that conversation had gone.

What bothered him even more, however, although he couldn't have said why, was how easily Claire fit in with the family, how quickly she caught on to the inside jokes flying fast and furious around the fully extended mahogany table. Merri had gotten on fine with his brothers and sisters, of course—and they, her—but he'd always felt like he'd needed to shield her from the full force of their exuberance.

Not Claire, though, who handily gave as good as she got, laughing and joking with the whole clan as if they'd all known each other for years. What was up with that?

Ethan hauled the platter with the turkey carcass into the kitchen, where the women were busy cleaning and divvying leftovers into a thousand plastic containers and gabbing a mile a minute. He'd only meant to dump the pulverized bird on the island, then haul *his* carcass to anyplace he didn't have to see Claire, who was at the sink rinsing dishes and handing them to Tyler's fiancée, Laurel, to put in the dishwasher. Because she was making him uncomfortable in ways he didn't even want to think about, was why.

Except then he noticed Kelly bouncing a wailing Jonathon, Laurel's ten-week-old, who wasn't in the least bit interested in being jostled out of his bad mood...which in turn brought back memories from when Ethan's own kids were infants, miserable for reasons known only to themselves....

"I've got this," Ethan said, plucking the kid from his startled sister-in-law's arms before booking it out of there, to somewhere, anywhere, where the women weren't. The family room was a no-go, however, since the space was crowded with guys—and his youngest sister Abby— cheering on the Eagles. Although at his soon-to-be step-son's cries, Tyler surged to his feet.

"You need me to take him?"

His youngest brother's concerned expression made Ethan's chest swell—who would have guessed that Tyler, the world's most dedicated bachelor, would hitch himself to a single mom with a newborn?

"No, we're good," Ethan said, tucking the baby against his chest as he also rejected the living room, filled with loud little boys playing video games. And the younger girls had vanished upstairs to play dress up with all the stuff Jeanne Noble had collected over the years for *her* little girls. Even the ones who'd only been passing through— for a few days, a few weeks, a couple of years—finding with the Nobles a haven from turbulence or uncertainty.

Some haven it was now, Ethan thought, pissed with himself for reacting to Claire like this. All the women who'd come on to him in the past three years—even the nice ones, the pretty ones, the reasonably normal ones—their attentions had slid right off, like water from an oiled deck. Then along comes this chick who wasn't even trying...

He didn't get it, he really didn't.

Finally, Ethan landed in the year-round sunroom off the dining room. The sun had long since gone to bed, but enough light filtered in from outside to keep the room from being completely dark. Settling with the baby in a cushioned wicker rocker, he began singing some silly little song that'd always soothed his own kids when they were fussy. Not that his singing voice was any great shakes, but if the kids hadn't cared, neither had he.

Jonny's wails gradually lost steam before the exhausted little guy finally passed out, slumped against Ethan's chest, and Ethan melded with the rocker as the infant did with him. He might have drifted off, too, except movement out of the corner of his eye made him start to attention. For a moment he assumed it was Laurel, come to collect her son, only to realize the shadowy figure was too short to be his future sister-in-law.

And her soft chuckle too raspy.

"The cute, it burns," she said.

"You can see us?"

"Heck, yeah."

He tried to sit up straighter, but nothing's heavier than a sleeping baby. "You're still here."

A beat or two preceded, "Got a problem with that?"

Ethan felt his cheeks tingle. "I was more thinking that you might. We're a pretty unruly bunch."

He heard her laugh. "I can handle unruly a little while longer, I think. Also, I'm too full to walk home."

"You walked?"

"Five blocks. Go, me." She paused, then said, "Want company?" and Ethan heard himself say, "Sure," and then she was perched on the edge of the chair nearest him, her hands curled around the edges of the striped cushion, her attention fixed on the baby. The weak light glanced off her curls, the side of her face. Through the leftover scent of the meal and burning logs, he caught a whiff of her perfume, something musky that tugged at a vulnerability he was too damned tired to argue with. Then he heard another gentle laugh.

"Omigosh—he's snoring?"

"They do that," he said, mentally shaking off an errant thought or six as he lowered his chin to smile at the baby. "One of the reasons Merri and I never coslept with the kids—they all made too much noise."

Claire tucked her hair behind her ear. In the nanosecond before it bounced back, he caught a glimpse of a tiny diamond stud, twinkling dully in the weak light. Her other earrings, they changed. But not that pair, nestled in her ears' upper curves—

"Your family's great."

"If borderline certifiable."

"That's what makes them great. I haven't laughed that much in a long, long time. Or felt…"

"What?"

"Good," she said, even though something told him that's not what she'd been about to say. "Like being in a living Normal Rockwell painting."

Ethan grunted. "We're hardly that."

"More than I ever had, that's for sure. It's a nice change." Another pause preceded, "You know, it occurs to me I've never held an infant."

"Seriously?"

"Nope. Babysat a few times as a teenager, but no actual babies."

"Wanna hold this one? I'm sure Laurel won't mind—"

"No, no… That's okay. Wouldn't want to disturb him, he looks so peaceful." She smiled again. "So do you."

Trick of the light, he wanted to say. Because if it was one thing he did not feel right now, it was peaceful.

Although no way in hell was he gonna let her see that.

"I can't believe it's been six years since I cuddled a little person like this," Ethan said quietly, gazing at his little nephew. "Since Bella. It really is one of the best feelings in the world."

* * *

Watching the big guy currently cuddling the tiny one, something tugged so hard inside Claire's chest she could barely breathe. Hard to believe this was the same dude who'd been bellowing at his players on the field earlier that day, who'd walked right into the middle of a fight outside the cafeteria the week before, prying apart a pair of Godzilla-size kids as if they were made of straw.

"I heard you singing, before."

"Poor you."

"Not at all." Because what he lacked in musicality, he more than made up for in sincerity. Suddenly antsy, Claire shifted in the chair. "Did you sing to your own kids?"

"To the twins and Bella, yeah. Jules would pass out right after she ate. No entertainment necessary. She was so laid-back Merri said she'd almost forget she was there. Good thing, too, since I was away so much, there at the beginning. But the boys..." He sighed. "Both of them were colicky, too. Like this one. Soon as the sun went down, they'd start crying. And they'd keep it up for hours. We'd no sooner get them both settled than somebody would rev up again."

"Gee. Fun times."

"I won't lie, for about six weeks there it was hell. I lost fifteen pounds." Chuckling, he added, "And Merri gained it. I don't think she ever forgave me *or* the boys for that."

"I don't blame her. Jeez." At his short laugh, she flushed. "Sorry, it just seems... I'm not sure I could handle that."

"Nobody is. Especially when you're in the middle of it. Six weeks seems like forever when you're so sleep deprived you can barely remember your name. But then they start crying less and laughing more, and you know what? In the greater scheme of things, a few sleepless nights are nothing. Of course, then they hit the Terrible Twos—"

"Oh, God, I can only imagine."

"—and you survive that, too. Because two-year-olds are funny as hell. And the hugs? Ah, man—there's nothing like 'em. And it only gets better..." He sighed. "Great. Now I sound like a freaking Hallmark card."

"Pretty much, yeah." Jonny stirred in his sleep; Ethan adjusted him on his chest, big hands cradling tiny bum and back, and Claire practically leaped from the chair and over to the French doors. Moonlight soaked the yard, making everything glow silver. "I can't believe how warm this room is," she said, grasping for a more neutral topic. "All these windows and not even a draft."

"Triple paned. And radiant heating underneath the tiles." Behind her, the chair faintly creaked. "It was my mom's favorite room. When she got sick, Dad had it completely weatherized so she could stay out here as long as she wanted, whenever she wanted. And he set up bird feeders all over the place, so she could watch them. The cardinals, especially, were her favorite."

Although Claire couldn't hear the sentimentality in his voice, she could sense it in his heart, beating soundly against a sleeping baby's ear. She cleared her throat, then said, "The rest of the house, too—speaking of Norman Rockwell. It's like... It feels so welcoming." She paused. "Safe."

"It was. Is."

"Almost seems a shame to sell it."

She heard Ethan sigh. "Can't say I'm not conflicted about that, frankly. It was Pop's and Mom's first home. *My* first home. Not to mention home to more foster kids than I can count. But it hasn't been the same since Mom died. For any of us, but Pop especially. He provided the protection, the sense of order and stability that some of those kids had never known before. But Mom..."

The chair creaked again. "She was the light," he said, his voice hushed. "The joy. For a long time I think Pop wanted to stay here because it reminded him of her. Now I think it only reminds him of what's missing. Not that he ever talks about it—I can't remember ever seeing him outwardly grieve, to be honest—but some things don't have to be put into words."

Now Claire heard it, even if only faintly: Ethan's own grief echoed in his reminiscence of his father. She turned, her arms crossed. "And you?" she said gently.

"Me?"

"Yeah. I can't imagine how hard it must be, still living in the house you shared with your wife. Heck, *I* can sense her presence there, and I didn't even know her—"

"Not even remotely the same situation," he said sharply, and she realized she'd overstepped.

"Sorry, I—"

"No," Ethan breathed out. "It's okay. Because to be honest, once the initial shock wore off I did consider finding us another place. For exactly the reasons you said. Hell, even after all this time I half expect her to walk into the family room, plop down beside me on the sofa. Or I'm gonna find her in the kitchen, making cookies or something. So at the beginning? I thought I'd go nuts, frankly. Except then I thought, it wasn't only about me, you know? That the kids... After what they'd just gone through, no chance to say goodbye, even..." He stopped, took a breath. "They needed consistency in their lives far more than I needed..." He paused again, and Claire though her heart would crack in two.

"Peace?"

His gaze briefly met hers before veering away again. "The kids... They come first. Always."

"So...you never do anything strictly for yourself?"

His laugh was dry. "At this point I'm not even sure what that would be."

"That's so sad."

"No, it's life," he said, more out of weariness, she thought, than as a rebuke. And, from years of digging into what makes a character tick, of analyzing literature up the wazoo, Claire thought maybe she heard a little warring going on inside his head—that his commitment to his kids' needs was perhaps taking more of a toll on his own that he'd admit. Or was ever likely to.

Which in turn reminded Claire of those months when, even though her primary focus had been making sure her mother was as comfortable and happy as possible, how often Mom would urge her to get out for a little while, go see a movie. Not that she did, or at least not very often. And during those last few weeks, never. But knowing she *could,* at least in theory—that she had permission to take care of *herself*—went a long way toward easing what, yes, had occasionally felt like a burden, even though she'd loved her mother with all her heart. So who was giving Ethan that same permission? To live not only his kids' lives but his own?

However, it wasn't her place to dispense advice she not only had no idea how to give but strongly suspected would be soundly rejected.

From way deep in the house, a roar went up. A touchdown, no doubt. Claire sat back down. "For what it's worth? I think you did the right thing, keeping the house."

His eyes again grazed hers for a moment before he looked back down at the baby. "Thanks." Then he stretched out his leg, as though it was bothering him.

"You okay?"

"What? Oh, yeah. Sure. Been sitting too long in this position, that's all." He smirked. "Yet another reminder that I'm not twenty-five anymore."

"I suppose… Maybe you could give me the baby to me for a bit? So you can get up, walk around."

"But I thought—"

"He looks harmless enough, asleep like that."

"Okay, then... Come here—" she stood, her stomach cramping "—and put one hand under his butt...that's right...and support his head with your other. You got it."

Awkwardly, she arranged the surprisingly floppy—and heavy—infant under her chin, then lowered herself back into the chair. "Like this?"

"Mostly. Although it's okay to breathe."

"You sure?"

"Positive," he said, pushing himself to his feet. Claire thought maybe she saw a grimace. And she definitely saw, once he started to move, a limp.

She eased back in the chair, amazed that the baby didn't wake up.

"See?" Ethan said. "Piece of cake, once you get the hang of it."

"Speak for yourself. This feels totally weird, holding a little human being."

"You never played with dolls?"

"No, actually. I liked building sets better. And yes, I was a strange kid."

He carefully worked his knee. "Bella prefers her brothers' toys to hers, too. Although her clothing choices make my teeth ache."

Claire smiled. And relaxed a little more. Then she said, "How bad is it?"

"How bad is what?"

"Your knee." When he frowned at her, she said, "Your dad told me you were hurt when you were overseas. And that you don't like talking about it."

Several beats passed before he said, "I was. And I don't. What I do is deal. You know, like a grown-up?"

"Got it. So...how'd you come to live with the Nobles? Or is that a forbidden subject, too?"

"Anybody ever tell you you're nosy?"

"I prefer *curious,* but yes. Often. Well?"

He shook his head, then sat back in the rocker, his leg stretched out in front of him as he massaged the muscles around his knee. "My parents were in their teens. Married, actually, but in way over their heads. Family Services convinced them to let the Nobles foster me, at least until they got their act together."

"How old were you?"

"Around two. Long story short, they never did work it out, and the Nobles adopted me. My birth parents eventually moved away, married other people, had other kids. I haven't heard from my father in years, although I'm still in touch with my birth mother. Occasionally. She and her second husband did come to my wedding, though. And she's seen the older kids, once or twice, although I doubt if they'd remember her."

"So...any half siblings?"

"Five. Three brothers, two sisters. But we're not close—"

"*There* you are!" Laurel said, scooting over to take her son from Claire, her smooth, straight hair curving around her face as she bent over. She lifted the sacked-out kid to her shoulder, making a little "aww" face when Jonny arched his back in his sleep. Claire wondered if she'd miss the feel of the baby in her arms...but honestly? Not so much.

"Game's over," Laurel said, "food's all sorted out, so the party's breaking up. Thanks for watching Jonny, you two." Then she turned to Claire. "Hey—Kelly and I are doing the Black Friday thing at the mall tomorrow morning... Wanna come with?"

"Oh! Wow. You know, I've never had the nerve to do that."

"Us, either," Laurel said with a grin. "So we can be Black Friday virgins together. Whaddya say? We can meet up here at, say, six—"

"In the *morning?*"

"Kelly says she'll bring the coffee and doughnuts. We'll go in her van. No guys, no kids… It'll be fun."

"Okay. Sure," Claire said, even as a little voice in her head said, *Are you off your rocker?* Then again, no guts, no glory. Or something.

"Great! See you then!" Laurel said, and she and Jonny were gone.

Ethan stood. "Guess that's our cue to make our retreat, too. You need a ride?"

"And again, five blocks. I also need to walk off the eighty pounds of food I put away. Kelly is seriously an amazing cook."

"Speaking of which, I almost forgot—there's something for you. In the kitchen."

"You mean besides the entire bag of leftovers Kelly insisted I take?"

"Yes." With that, he headed out of the sunroom, his gait a little stiff, clearly expecting her to follow. The kitchen was empty, the dishwasher whirring away, the only lights still on the pendants over the island. He ducked into the pantry, returning with a pie box…and a slightly embarrassed smile.

"I remembered what you said about eating a whole pumpkin pie by yourself. So this is all for you."

A laugh burst from her throat. "What did you do, steal it?"

"No, I asked first. So." He held out the box. "Here."

This was silly, it was only a pie, but… Claire carefully set the box in the plastic bag she'd left earlier on the counter, on top of all the other food Kelly had foisted on her. "Why?" she quietly asked, not looking at him.

"I guess…to say thank-you for taking the boys this morning. Although since I didn't make the thing I'm not sure how much it counts."

KAREN TEMPLETON   *111*

Smiling, she hefted the bag off the counter and faced him again. "You thought of me. So it counts." *Big-time.*

"Um...you sure you don't need a ride?"

Okay, so she might have been tilting a little. "Honestly, it's not that heavy—"

A somewhat breathless Juliette burst into the kitchen. "Kelly says you guys are going to the mall tomorrow?"

"It would appear so—"

"Can I come, too? Please?" She turned to her father. "*Please,* Dad?"

"If it's okay with Kelly and Laurel. And Claire—"

"Hey, I'm only going along for the ride. If everyone else is cool—"

"I already asked, they totally are! Omigod, this is going to be so much fun—!"

Behind her, Ethan groaned. She looked back to see him shaking his head at his daughter's vapor trail. "Definitely her mother's child. Merri also never met a bargain she didn't love. Put the kid in an entire mall of bargains..." He shuddered, and Claire laughed.

Which actually brought forth something close to a real smile.

And that, boys and girls, was worth any amount of Black Friday madness.

Chapter Seven

Thank goodness Ethan actually didn't have anything on his agenda today—other than getting up the outside decorations before the kids blew a gasket—because considering the sleepless night he'd had? He was basically worth bupkes.

Because what was going on here, he thought as he put on coffee, then stared at the maker as if he expected it to tell his fortune, went beyond deprivation-driven, half-assed fantasies. Which was not good. Or fair. To anybody. Which naturally only made him feel guilty that he was thinking about Claire Jacobs *that way.* Although the truth was he'd been feeling *that way* about her for some time, but only in the occasional moment when his defenses were down and other things…weren't.

Beside him, Barney yipped, then sat and gave Ethan sad eyes. As if he wanted some coffee, too. Or, more likely, a doggie treat. Ethan reached for the Milk-Bone bag in the cupboard, handed one over without making the dog perform. Barney cocked his head, suspicious.

"No strings. I swear."

Cautiously, the dog took the treat, then pranced out of the room before The Man could change his mind. Ethan poured his coffee as he yawned, taking a sip before it'd cooled off. Wincing, he carried the cup to the kitchen table, yanked out a chair and dropped into it, remembering sitting at another kitchen table at around fourteen or so, when he and the Colonel had had a surprisingly blunt chat about those things that, like every other teenage boy in the world, Ethan thought about pretty much constantly. And the takeaway was, a *real* man was in charge, in control, of both his thoughts and his body.

His life.

Of course, that last part was a joke. Monkey wrenches happened. To some more than others. But if he couldn't control his destiny—or, it would seem, a certain body part—he could still control his reactions. His choices. And, make no mistake, he did have choices. A few, anyway. And one of those choices was to never again let another human being—save the possible exception of his children—have that much power over his emotions.

Jules came bouncing into the kitchen, dressed like an elf—red tights, green shorts, black-and-white striped vest over a sparkly red sweater. She was even wearing earrings with bells, good God. Only thing missing was the pointy-toed shoes, which she'd apparently eschewed in favor of her brown suede hiking boots. And the streak, conspicuously absent from her just-washed hair.

"Whatever happened to jeans and hoodies?" Ethan grumbled as she poured herself a glass of orange juice.

"Um...I don't want to look like everybody else?"

"Aren't you worried somebody'll take away your teenager membership card?"

"Har-har. And besides, I can't very well be an actress if I'm afraid to stand out, right? Grab someone's attention?"

"And whose attention, exactly, do you expect to attract at the mall?" he said, immediately realizing, at his daughter's blush, that he'd inadvertently hit a bull's-eye. Well, crap.

"Nobody, silly Daddy," she said, swooping in to give him a hug as a horn beeped outside. "That's Miss Jacobs, gotta go—"

"And you both can hold your horses a minute," Ethan said, getting to his feet, only to remember he was still in his sleep pants and an ancient Marine Corps T-shirt. Then he thought, *Screw it, I'm sure she's seen worse,* and padded after his daughter through the living room and outside onto the cold, cold step. Barefoot.

Claire lowered her window as his daughter jingled out to the car and climbed in beside her.

"Fetching," she said, grinning. His arms crossed over his chest, Ethan came to the edge of the step. His knee complained loudly. As did his rapidly freezing feet.

"It's six-freaking-thirty in the morning, I'm not exactly holding court. You really ready for this?"

"I sincerely doubt it. But there will be doughnuts, so it's all good."

"Got your phone, Jules?" he called out, even though he couldn't see her. Claire laughed.

"She rolled her eyes. I'm gonna guess that's a yes." Then she pushed a curl behind her ear, the tiny diamond twinkling at him as she said, "You should join us for lunch in the courtyard," and he could hear his daughter's groan. "All of you, I mean. Bring Bella to see Santa."

"You kidding? Bella ditched Santa when she was four."

Claire jerked her thumb to her side. "Got that in stereo. But you should still come. You know, join the party. Have some fun."

Only the presence of his already jaded daughter kept

him from asking her what she'd been smoking. "At a shop-ping mall on Black Friday?"

"Good point."

"Anyway, today's when I deck the outside of the house. It's a tradition."

Claire glanced up at the thick, nasty-looking clouds hunched overhead, clearly ready to barf all over his plans, then back at him. "Oh, yeah?"

"Eh, this'll blow off by noon."

"Whatever you say," she said with another light laugh, then shifted the car's gears. "We'll be back when our money, sanity or legs give out. Whichever comes first."

Then, with a little wave, she pulled out of the driveway, Jules yammering beside her. Only, for a moment it was Merri driving, his little girl yakking away in that silly hat she used to have with the flaps like dog's ears covering her cheeks, the two of them going off to have a little "girl time." And his heart ached.

But whether because it was cracking, or stretching, he wasn't entirely sure.

"Honestly, this is worse than Times Square!" Claire said, dodging yet another woman in faux fur and spandex who clearly considered the entire mall her personal space.

Beside her, Laurel—who'd done her own time in the city—pushed out a dry laugh. "Truly. Oh, for pity's sake... *Kelly!*" she yelled over the blare of some pop star's pa-thetic rendition of "Winter Wonderland," as the redhead zoomed ahead like a guided missile, energy fairly sparking from her bright, wavy hair. Claire checked behind them to make sure Juliette, who'd been plugged into her phone for the past hour, was keeping up. Because Ethan would probably not take kindly to Claire's losing the child. "For God's sake, Kell," Laurel yelled again, coming to a dead halt. "*Stop,* already!"

Even though she was ready to drop, too, Claire chuckled. Four hours, she'd been with these women, and while they were each a different brand of crazy, the flavors seemed to blend quite nicely. At least well enough to endure a two-hundred-store mall on Black Friday. Although clearly Laurel, her posture as limp as her straight brown hair, had reached her limit.

Shopping bags from a half dozen stores clutched in her hands, Kelly turned, clearly puzzled. "What?"

Laurel plunked down on a bench beside a cluster of totally incongruous tropical plantings—even more incongruously embellished with Christmas ornaments the size of small planets—blissfully soaking up the dreary light from the three-story-high skylight overhead. Her own back none too happy either, Claire joined her, leaving Juliette to roll her eyes before dropping onto another bench a discreet ten feet away to continue her electronic communication with half the free world. With a sigh, Kelly trudged back.

"You guys are total wusses," she said, and Laurel snorted.

"Yeah, well, your boobs aren't about to explode," she said in a low voice. Although with the roar of shoppers surging around them like the Jersey turnpike at rush hour, it wasn't like anyone would hear them. Or care. "And no, I wasn't about to schlep my pump out here to go sit in some ladies' room lounge to express milk. And how is it you're like the Energizer Bunny, O Pregnant One?"

"Second trimester," Kelly said with a shrug. "That hallowed window between being perpetually sick and perpetually winded. I could probably keep going for another three hours—"

"Jules! Hey!"

Almost grateful for a diversion from a conversation she couldn't relate to, Claire looked over to see a gaggle of kids from Hoover zeroing in on them, with Rosie—

wearing a Santa hat set at a rakish angle—at the head of the pack. Mostly the drama kids, Claire now saw. Including the ever-elusive Scott…sans the ever-present Amber. Huh. She glanced at Juliette, who was doing the deer-in-headlights thing, and thought, *Oh, dear, this will never do.*

"Hey, Miss Jacobs!" Rosie said, radiating enough Christmas spirit to light up the entire state. "Julie said you guys were coming here, but I didn't think we'd see you! Cool, huh?"

"It is," she said, then introduced the girl to Laurel and Kelly. "Did you all…come together?"

"Nah, Mom dropped me off, and then I ran into Shawna, and then we somehow started collecting the others. Like a snowball going down a hill," she said with a chuckle… and a telling glance toward Juliette. Uh-huh.

But whatever. Claire turned to her charge and said, "You should join your friends," which earned her the buggiest blue eyes in teen history, as well as a stammered, "I…um…"

"Yeah, you should totally come with," Rosie said to Juliette, nodding a little too vigorously. "We were headed for the food court, in fact. Mom said she'd pick me up whenever—" Rosie turned back to Claire "—but I'm sure she'd be cool with getting Julie home, too."

"Fine with me. But you should probably check with your dad, honey, make sure it's okay with him—"

"Oh, I'm sure it is," the brunette said, "since it's not like we've never been here by ourselves before."

"Still, he needs to know there's been a change of plans." Then Claire looked at Juliette, whose expression was such a mixture of hopeful and terror stricken that Claire's heart went out to her. "Unless you'd rather stay with us?" she said, touching her shoulder.

Her braces glinting as she caught her lower lip between her teeth, Juliette darted a look at Rosie, then at Scott—

dark haired, dimpled and totally engrossed in a convo with two of his compadres—then back at Rosie. Finally, with what Claire guessed were very clammy hands, the girl punched at her phone, then turned away from the group. Seconds later she handed the phone to Claire.

"He wants to talk to you."

Claire took the phone, plugging her finger into her other ear so she could hear. "You need me to corroborate her story?"

"I'm the father of a fifteen-year-old girl, what do you think?"

"That you're a very *good* father of a fifteen-year-old girl. But it's true. Rosie's here, she somehow accumulated a batch of kids—"

"Yeah, that sounds about right."

"And it's only for an hour or so." She decided against mentioning The Boy, partly because she sincerely doubted this was an issue, partly because the kids were traveling in a herd. Like wildebeests on the African plains. And she'd trust Rosie in a zombie apocalypse, let alone in a mall teeming with Jerseyites.

"You'll still be there?"

"Um, actually, I'm not sure. Hold on…" She looked from Kelly to Laurel. "So are we staying or going?"

Shrugging, Kelly nodded at Laurel the Limp. "Up to you."

That got a sigh. "I really did want to check out Macy's before we left. Maybe if I…" She grimaced at her chest. "If I could maybe find a cup or something?"

"We will find you a cup or something," Kelly said, tugging the other woman to her feet. "Trust me, I am an expert on these things. And don't even give me smack about 'wasting it,' there's plenty more where that came from. Also, I need lunch. Like, yesterday…"

Laughing, Claire said into the phone. "I guess we're

staying. And it looks like we're all headed for the food court, so we won't be far. I'll keep an eye on her, I promise."

She heard a heavy sigh, then a weary laugh. "I know I can't protect her 24/7, but…"

"Hey. You've got nothing on my dad, who I half expected to move to New York *with* me. And I was twenty-two, not fifteen. And yes, it made me nuts. Then. But there's a lot worse things in the world than having someone give a damn about you. So don't worry about it, I've got it covered."

Silence buzzed between for a moment before he said, "Thanks."

"No problem," she said, then handed the phone back to Juliette. A minute later, the kids all shuffled off to the food court as Claire and the others followed at a respectful, unobtrusive distance. The kids commandeered a table or three closest to the Burger King while the ladies decided on Chinese food. After telling the others what she wanted, Laurel—purloined soft drink cup in hand—hustled off to the ladies' room, leaving Kelly and Claire alone at their table with enough food to *feed* China.

"So what's going on with Jules and the hottie?" Kelly said, shoveling in orange chicken at the speed of light.

Claire frowned at her. "Hottie?"

"Shaggy dark hair? Killer smile? Who she keeps staring at like a kid in a toy store?"

"Who, you will notice, is not returning her stares."

"In all likelihood because she's probably creeping him out. Seriously…do we need to do an intervention here?"

"Like I'd have any clue how to do that," Claire said with snort. "In high school? That was me, the one rendered mute any time a boy looked at me."

"Yeah, me, too," Kelly said, sighing and shoveling simultaneously. Talented. "Who we need is Sabrina. Matt's sister," she said at Claire's frown. "I swear, boys would follow her with their tongues hanging out. So gross. Fascinating, but gross."

"So you guys all went to school together?"

Nodding, Kelly bit off half an egg roll. "Sabrina, Matt and I were in the same grade. I lived next door, but I spent most of my waking hours at the Nobles'. And a fair amount of my sleeping hours, too, actually."

"So you and Matt...?"

"Didn't happen until later." Her eyes twinkled. "*Much* later. Like less than a year ago."

"Get out."

"It's true. Ethan and Merri, though... Joined at the hip from the time they were fifteen or something."

"Wow."

The rest of the egg roll disappeared. "Sabrina and I thought it was all terribly romantic," Kelly said, chewing. "Well, after we got past being scandalized. What can I say, we were ten. We couldn't even imagine kissing, let alone anything else." Then, swallowing, she laughed. "Okay, I take that back. *I* couldn't imagine kissing. Bree... I don't even want to know what she was imagining back then."

Claire smiled. She'd already gathered from Kelly that Sabrina was what her grandmother, now long gone, would've called a "pistol." She forked in a bite of her own sweet-and-sour pork and asked, "What was she like? Merri, I mean." When Kelly arched an eyebrow, Claire said, "I have her kid in two of my classes, I'm curious what her mom was like."

Kelly gave her a "whatever you say, chickie" look, then shrugged. "Blond. Adorable. Very sweet, as I recall. But genuine. I moved away when I was sixteen, after Ethan had left for the marines, but before that I remember him being so...devoted to her. Not like your average teenage boy, that was for sure."

"So he really was the high school football star?" Kelly shot her a glance. "His dad indicated he was very talented."

"He really was. Next to Merri, football was his life. Matt played, too—and he was pretty good—but he wasn't consumed by it like Ethan was. He'd even been courted by a couple of major schools. I mean, *major* schools. Notre Dame, Ohio State. Yeah. He was that good. We're talking full-ride scholarships, the works."

"Then, what…?"

"He decided to go into the marines instead. I have no idea why, although I guess he figured he could still play when his six years were up. Who knows. Except…"

"He got hurt."

"Exactly. Then Merri turned up pregnant, so they got married…" She shrugged. "I wasn't around, I only know what I've heard from Matt and Bree. All I can say is, though—I've never known anybody able to make lemonade out of lemons like that man. The way he is with his kids… He should give lessons. Seriously."

"You should hear how his players talk about him."

"Yeah?"

"I swear, they practically worship the man. I gather he doesn't let 'em get away with crap, but he's always there for them, too. Especially the ones who maybe don't have somebody there for them all the time. Or ever, really."

Kelly gave her a funny look. "You got a soft spot for the guy?"

"Who wouldn't?" she said, knowing full well what Kelly was asking and honestly not caring. "After everything he's been through… He's something else."

"Yes," Kelly said. "Yes, he is…."

Yakking into her phone, Laurel reappeared…but she didn't sit. "Yeah, okay, but it'll take me a minute to get there." Her voice went all mushy. "Me, too, baby. See you in a few."

She dropped her phone back into her purse, then consolidated some of her purchases to free up a plastic bag, which she then loaded with her own take-out containers. "Ty and Little Stuff are over at Sears, he needs some tools, or something—Ty, not the baby—so I said I'd meet them, go home from there. That okay with you guys?"

"Sure—"

"Of course—"

Smiling, she leaned over and gave each of them a quick hug, then waved over to Juliette...whose wave back wasn't exactly all happy-happy-fun-fun. Hmm.

"She okay?" Laurel asked.

"I thought she was," Claire said, then smiled for Laurel. "But you go on, we've got it covered."

"You sure...?"

"Absolutely," Kelly said with a sharp nod, even as her eyes darted to Claire.

"Okay...call me!" Laurel said to Kelly before she scooted off like a pack mule on speed. A moment later Claire noticed Juliette glance in their direction again, then get up from the table to dump her trash in the garbage bin, her lower lip quivering.

"Damn," Kelly muttered.

"Exactly. Should we...?"

"She knows we're here if she needs us. It'll be okay."

Claire looked at Ethan's sister-in-law, who was finally slowing down with the food consumption. "So how do you know when to stick your nose in and when to let things unfold on their own?"

Her laugh was dry. "Nobody *knows*. We all make it up as we go along. And anyone who tells you otherwise is lying. Also, my kids are ten, three and still inside. I do not know from teenagers. Parenting them, anyway. However, I remember my own teen years vividly—"

Claire sighed. "Don't we all?"

"So sad, right? But from the little I've been around Juliette, I gather she's one of those kids who needs to work out stuff on her own. She's also a lot tougher than I was at that age."

"Me, too," Claire said, following the kid's unenthusiastic return to the table, then her short conversation with her friend, who frowned at the oblivious Scott still yukking it up with one of the other guys. After a moment, Rosie nodded, standing to give Juliette a hug before the girl started back toward them. Kelly's eyes cut to Claire's again before she smiled up at Juliette.

"What's up, kiddo?"

"Nothing," she said with a shrug as she slumped onto the seat beside Claire, her hands stuffed into her vest pockets. Claire nudged the container of egg rolls toward her, but she shook her head. "They want to hit up a lot of stores we already did, so I decided…" Claire saw her swallow before she flashed a fake smile. "I can't believe I'm saying this, but I'm seriously wiped out. You think we can go soon?"

"Of course," Kelly said, gathering her shopping bags, the leftover food, as Claire did the same. "We've got three more Saturdays before Christmas, plenty of time…"

Twenty uncomfortably quiet minutes later, they were back at the Colonel's, everything transferred to Claire's car so she could take the girl home. As the silence continued, however, after they were once more on the road, Claire finally couldn't stand it anymore.

"Wanna talk about it?"

And the floodgates opened.

"Forget *t-talking* to me, he wouldn't even *look* at me!" Juliette said, scrubbing tears off her cheeks. Mad tears, Claire decided, given both how tightly the girl clamped her arms across her chest and the furious set to her mouth. "What a *jerk!*"

"Well...you were with a large group, maybe he didn't realize—"

"Oh, he realized. He *knew*." The arms tightened. "He simply didn't want to acknowledge my pr-presence. Never mind that we—"

A chill skedaddled down Claire's spine. "That you what?"

"Nothing."

"Julie, for heaven's sake—"

"He kissed me, okay?"

"What? When—?"

"Tuesday. During rehearsal, when neither of us were onstage. There's this little janitor's room or something backstage—"

"Yes, I know it. Go on."

A heavy sigh preceded, "Scott'd been kind of flirting with me all afternoon. During rehearsal, I mean. I thought I was imagining it at first, but Rosie said, no, he was definitely coming on to me, I should totally go for it. Especially since everybody knew he'd broken up with Amber. So he was, you know. Free. In theory, anyway. Then he slipped me a note to meet him backstage.…" She pushed out another sigh. "I am *such* an idiot. Because he was only... What do you call that?"

"Using you?" Claire said gently.

"Yeah. And you know what the worst part was? It was my first kiss. So now *that* moment's ruined forever."

If Claire hadn't been driving, she would have shut her eyes. Since she was, the best she could do was blow out a sigh of her own. Juliette glanced at her, then started gnawing on a hangnail before she caught herself, jerked her hand back to her lap.

"And you don't have to lecture me, I know what I did.… It was stupid. I don't mean kissing him, although that wasn't real bright. I mean, letting him get me alone like that."

"So…nothing else happened? I mean, he didn't—"

"Nothing. I swear. In fact, I think Scott realized how dumb it was the same time I did. He even apologized. Yes, really. But Dad would still have a cow if he knew."

"More like an entire herd," Claire murmured. Beside her, she heard a small laugh. But it wasn't funny, and Claire could only be grateful that it had only been a kiss. Because while in an ideal world boundaries were not only acknowledged, but respected, in the *real* world asshats happened, and boys who should—but for whatever reason didn't—know better far too often mistook vulnerability for opportunity. And, sadly, not to display their better sides.

Even so, Claire said, "Just don't blame yourself for what happened. Because Scott did use you, probably to salve his own ego. No matter what, that was wrong."

"Duh," Jules said, digging in her purse for a tissue to blow her nose. "Even so, nobody told me to go with him, to put myself in that situation. Especially since—the other stuff aside—I knew he was still hung up on Amber. I mean seriously, they broke up like five minutes ago…. *God.* I'm usually smarter than that. A lot smarter—"

"And do you realize," Claire said as they pulled into the girl's driveway, "how many times you've put yourself down in the past thirty seconds?"

Juliette's head swung around, her eyes huge. Up on a ladder, Ethan was stringing lights while the boys raked up the last of the leaves. "It's a trap, sweetie," Claire said. "Making mistakes is how we learn. All of us. Has nothing to do with how smart we are—"

"It's okay," the girl said, swiping at her eyes. "I'm fine now. Really."

Of course you are, Claire thought, cutting the engine. Despite Juliette's obvious need to vent, clearly she wasn't looking to Claire for either sympathy or advice. Then again, she was probably taking her cues from her dad. Didn't take a psychology degree to figure out this was not a family big on exposing their weak spots. Or asking for help.

Which, oddly, rankled a little. Never mind that Claire did not need or want some teenage girl looking to her for answers she sure as hell didn't have. And probably never would. So, by rights, she should feel immensely relieved.

Not…hurt.

Squelching the idiocy, Claire popped the trunk and got out of the car to help Juliette with her purchases as Ethan descended the ladder, outfitted in jeans, a faded New York Giants hoodie and a string of lights. The big, old-fashioned ones now back in vogue.

"Hey, pumpkin," he said to his daughter, his brow immediately furrowing when she wouldn't look at him as she hauled her bags from the trunk. "Wow. You leave anything in the mall for the other people?"

"Ha-ha," Juliette said with all the oomph of flat soda, and Claire wanted to say, *If that's how you play "fine," cutie-pie, your acting skills need work.* From across the street, a boy about the twins' age called over, asking if they wanted to come play video games. Rakes in hand, the guys looked over at their dad, eager as puppies. Ethan waved them off, the rakes clattering to the ground as he returned his gaze to his daughter.

"Wanna help me put up the lights?"

"Actually…I think I'm going to take a nap. The mall totally wore me out."

"Um…sure, baby. No problem." But the instant she was inside, Ethan's eyes swung to Claire's. "Kid hasn't napped since she was three. So what happened?"

Maybe Juliette wasn't looking to her for answers, but right now her father was. And wasn't that just dandy? Since being caught in the middle was her favorite place to be. And, based on Ethan's expression, she had approximately five seconds to decide what to do about it.

Although the kiss… That, Claire would keep to herself. For now, anyway. The kid was mad, and her ego had taken it on the chin, but she wasn't traumatized. Those signs, Claire knew. Not from her own experience, thank God, but from classmates, friends. So right or wrong, she was making a judgment call to not send Ethan over the edge about something Claire sure as heck wouldn't have wanted *her* father to know about.

The rest of the story, though, she didn't feel right about keeping to herself, whether it pissed Juliette off or not. Ethan deserved to know as much as possible about what was going on in her daughter's head. Otherwise, how could be the kind of father he obviously wanted to be?

Shivering, she slammed shut the trunk. "You got an extra sweatshirt or something? I could help, if you want."

"While you talk?"

"You bet."

He gave her a seriously distrustful look, then nodded. "Coming right up," he said, disappearing inside, and Claire let out a long, long breath.

Chapter Eight

Pawing through his closet—God knew nothing of Jules's would fit Claire, even though they were about the same height—Ethan irritably mused about how women never thought a guy was sensitive/intuitive/whatever enough to figure out when they were keeping a secret. Granted, the man might not have a clue what the secret was—or, in many cases, the desire or energy to find out—but the signs were obvious, if you knew what to look for.

And Ethan knew those signs, boy. Backward, forward and inside out. Because he'd made it his business to learn them.

Grunting, he yanked out another sweatshirt, giving it a quick sniff test before returning outside, handing it over.

"Thanks," she said, wriggling it over her vest, then tugging her curls free. She looked absolutely ridiculous. Especially since her legs looked like rolls of gift wrap. Snowmen and reindeer? Really? "Where's the little one?" she asked, folding up the sleeves.

"With Abby, my youngest sister." He glanced up at the house. "So this will be a surprise."

"Aw, that's sweet. So tell me what to do."

"Those lights by the front steps? They need to be untangled. And the longer you avoid the subject," he said to her Frosty and Rudolph–stamped posterior when she bent over to pick up the wadded coil, "the more I'm gonna assume you're trying to decide which parts of the truth to share. This isn't my first rodeo, you know."

She stood, shaking out the string. "Although Juliette is your first teenager."

"That I spawned, yeah. That I lived with?" He shook his head. "Trust me, after Sabrina's shenanigans? I think I can handle Juliette's. As long as I know what I'm dealing with."

The lights delicately clacked as she shook them a little harder, then squinted over at him. "Is there *anything* you feel you can't handle? That, you know, might be outside the realm of your expertise?"

He felt a flash of…something. Irritation? Surprise? Amusement, maybe? "And why would I admit it if there were?"

"Maybe because it would make you more… What's that word? Oh, yeah. *Human.*"

"Oh, believe me…I'm plenty human." She bent over again, and the reindeer and snowmen tangoed, and he thought, *You should only know how human I am.* "But I've also got four kids depending on me to be the one in control. The one they can count on."

The plug end of the string finally freed, Claire set it on the ground and started walking backward, gradually working loose the rest of the lights. "That's a lot of pressure you're putting on yourself," she said so quietly he almost missed it.

"Only handling what life's tossed in my lap. So. You gonna tell me what's wrong with my little girl?"

"Yeah." She carefully gathered up the untangled string to set it on the top step. "She's not a *little* girl anymore. She's a big girl. With big-girl issues."

That spot at the base of his skull? Cramped like a son of a bitch. He glanced up at Juliette's window, then back at Claire. "Meaning...boys?" he said in a low voice.

At least her smile was sympathetic. "It was bound to happen sooner or later."

He scrubbed a hand over his head, then pushed out a sigh. "I was hoping for later."

"You and every other father on the face of the planet." The tiny diamonds in her ears played peekaboo with her wind-tossed hair as she came closer. "She's gonna hate me for telling you this, but...there's this boy she likes in the play—"

"Who?"

"Never mind, it's immaterial. Yes, it is," she said to his glare. "Anyway, he had a girlfriend, but they broke up, and I guess Julie thought maybe she had a chance. Except then today—"

"Today? He was at the mall?"

"With all those other kids, yeah. Remember, she called you?"

"Right." He frowned. "But she didn't say anything about a boy."

Claire gave him a "oh, you poor thing" look, then said very patiently, "Of course she didn't. Because she knew you'd do exactly what you're doing—"

"But you knew about it?"

"Ethan. Get a grip. We're talking a dozen kids at least. Including Rosie. *Nothing was going to happen.* Except, well... Long story short, said boy totally ignored your daughter. And she took it hard. And *please* don't tell me that was a sigh of relief."

"You bet it was. She's only fifteen, for God's sake—"

"And *how* old were you and Merri when you first starting going together?"

Heat pricked at his cheeks. "Totally different thing."

"No, Ethan. It's not. Except that I gather it was mutual between you guys from the beginning. In this case, not so much. Actually, not at all. So you're worrying about nothing. Except the one thing you should be concerned about, which is that your daughter's feelings got hurt today. So be kind."

Ethan narrowed his eyes at Claire, a trick that usually, and quickly, unearthed any hidden truths the object of his scrutiny might be inclined to hide. But she only lifted her brows and said, "What?"

Cool customer, that Claire.

"So you're telling me she looked like that simply because some dude didn't want to talk to her?"

"Actually, she looked like that because she was mad at herself for being upset that he didn't talk to her."

"I assume that was supposed to make sense."

"To anyone with estrogen pumping through their veins, it does. And by the way? If you think for a second I would have *let* anything happen to her, your head's up your butt a lot farther than I thought. What nobody can prevent, though—not even you—is her getting her heart bruised. Even broken. Probably more than once. And yes, I know I've got no business getting up in yours, but tough. Look, I can tell you—and Merri—have given Juliette all the tools she needs to handle whatever life throws at her. But what good are they if you don't let her use them?"

Okay, so maybe *cool* wasn't exactly the right word.

Logically he should be pissed that she *had* gotten in his face, lecturing him on things that were none of her concern. Except, for one thing, she was more right than he wanted to admit. And for another, it took guts to say that stuff. And that he liked.

He liked it a lot.

Still, it seemed prudent to glare at her for another few seconds—you know, to keep things straight between them—before he lowered himself to the small landing in front of the door. "I can't help wanting to protect my kids, Claire."

"Oh, for pity's sake..." She blew out a breath. "Of course not. You'd be a pretty crummy dad if you didn't. But..."

She sat beside him, her perfume mingling with the scent of fireplace smoke and a neighbor's burning leaves, intoxicatingly exotic and earthy at the same time. "My father was überprotective, too," she said, her hands plugged into the sweatshirt's pockets as she looked out over the yard. "Especially since not only was I a girl, but his only child. Hovering? The man had it *down*. And in some ways—a lot of ways, actually—I loved him for it. Because I always felt safe. Except..."

Her curls quivered when she shook her head. "But by the time I got to high school, I was like this precious little snowflake that would melt if somebody looked at me wrong. Because Dad's wanting to keep me from getting hurt meant he never let me try anything he thought *might* hurt me. Like find my own way, or use my own noggin to figure things out. Like the world would end if I made a mistake. So I had no clue how to deal with anything, you know? Meaning I also had zero self-confidence. And that blew. Big-time."

"And yet...you went to New York?"

"Yeah. After four years of college, at least three of which were spent majoring in How to Grow a Pair. In that respect, Jules is light-years ahead of me." Finally, she looked at him. "She's going to make some iffy choices, Ethan. Stumble and fall and get a few owies. Because that's how humans grow and learn and become adults. But as long as she knows you've got her back, she'll be okay."

Ethan frowned. "I don't understand. You just said—"

"There's a difference between supporting Jules by showing her how to navigate all the crap life's going to throw in her path and trying to clear it for her." Looking away again, she said, "Because, believe me, there's no place in today's world for a pansy-assed woman."

Certainly couldn't argue with that, could he? But still...

"I never thought this would be a cakewalk. In fact, those first few weeks after Merri..." He rubbed the center of his chest where the ache still throbbed, if faintly. "I'm not a big one for praying, but there were nights when I'd lie awake for hours thinking, over and over and over, 'Please don't let me screw this up.'"

Out of the corner of his eye, he caught Claire's smile. "If it makes you feel any better, I'd say your prayer's being answered."

"Is it?" He linked his hands between his knees. "Merri was...easy," he said, then pushed a short laugh through his nose. "As in, uncomplicated. Easy to get along with. To understand. She never played games. Especially those guessing games so many guys complain about, where their wives or girlfriends let them know there's an issue, then expect them to figure it out on their own."

"Yeah, I never got that, either," Claire said, squinting into the sun. "Kind of hard to have a relationship—a real one, anyway—if you're not up-front with the other person. I mean...that's just respect, you know?"

"And you call yourself a Jersey girl," he said, and she laughed.

"There's different shades of Jersey. 'In your face' isn't necessarily the same as being honest. At least not with yourself. A girl can hide a boatload of insecurities behind the drama." She chuckled again. "Not to mention the makeup."

Ethan smiled, then said, "Jules said you'd been married?"

"I was, yeah. For about five minutes, a million years ago."

"What happened?"

She curled forward to brush dirt off her boot, then hugged her knees. "Nothing terrible, it simply didn't work. Probably because it should've never happened to begin with. Nobody's fault, really, that we got swept up in the fantasy. And Brad's a nice guy. He remarried, in fact, last summer. The right girl this time. I hope so, anyway. He deserves to be happy. He did not, however, deserve me."

His forehead cramped. "What makes you say that?"

Claire looked at him, a smile pushing at one side of her mouth. "And why should that matter to you?"

"Because it sounds like you're putting yourself down—"

She made a choking sound. "Say what?"

"You heard me. And that's not right. Because you don't seem like a terrible person or anything. A little crazy, maybe," he said, which got another light laugh, "but not off the rails. You don't think you deserve good things, too?"

"That's not what I said. Or meant, anyway. Because what Brad did deserve was somebody who was all in. Not someone who felt…crowded. Like suddenly… How do I explain this?" She frowned for a moment. "I felt like I was supposed to be part of a whole—which totally works for some people, don't get me wrong—rather than being whole on my own. Which felt…weird. And uncomfortable. Especially after how hard I'd fought to ditch the insecurities. And it wasn't fair to him, living with someone who kept catching herself wondering when he was going to go home and get out of my space."

"Ouch."

"Exactly. And the thing was, I did love him. Or thought I did. But the whole point of loving someone is wanting to be with them, right? Instead, I realized it was bugging me, that he was always…there. So then I felt guilty about what I was feeling, and…things went downhill from there."

"But didn't you have roommates?"

"And I hated every minute of it, believe me. But at least I always had my own bed, in my own bedroom. And yes, I paid more for the privilege. I could *almost* share the kitchen and bathroom without going nuts, but sharing a closet? Oh, hell, no." Her eyes slid to his. "And I assume from that look on your face you're no longer so sure about my not being off the rails."

"Actually, now that I think about it, those things on your legs kinda already made that point."

She stretched out one leg, admiring. "Hey. They make me happy."

"As I was saying."

Unfazed, she lowered her foot again, then said, "So you never, ever feel like you want a little Ethan time? Away from the kids, I mean."

"No."

She snorted.

"Okay, sometimes. I am human. Despite your doubts about that."

"You sure?"

"Mostly, yeah," he said with a slight smile. "But I never felt that way about Merri. In fact, one of the things…" He stopped, took a breath. "One of the things I most miss is how having her in my life… I never felt alone. Even when we were apart, she was there. Here," he said, pressing a hand into his chest.

"That must've been nice," Claire said softly.

"It was. What you said? About feeling part of a whole? That's exactly what it was like. Except…" Sighing, he rubbed his head. "It was even more than that. Because it wasn't like we leaned on each other, or needed each other to function. But we were… I don't know. Better together than we were individually, I guess. A real team. In every sense of the word."

Claire rested her cheek in her hand. "Would you want that again?"

He got to his feet, grabbing the abandoned lights to start stringing them along hooks he'd put up the first Christmas after they'd moved in. "Not something I let myself think about. And anyway…" Ethan looped the strand through the next hook, then the one after that. "Kinda got my hands full with the kids. My job. And we're finally doing okay. Good, even. Why would I want to shake things up? Hand me that next string, would you?"

Claire grabbed the coiled string from behind her, then stood to carry it over to him. "Thanks," he muttered, reaching for the strand without looking. Only his fingers brushed hers, and he jerked at how icy they were, before frowning down to see that the tip of her nose, her cheeks, were red from the cold, and something inside him…shifted. Almost imperceptibly, for sure, but he'd definitely felt it. Yes, despite everything she'd said, and everything *he'd* said, and those crazy-ass things on her legs, and her taking his daughter's side about being an actress…

He trusted her, he realized. With everything he had in him. Because she *didn't* play games, or do the coy, cutesy thing that drove him bonkers. So if nothing else, whatever was going on here… It was real. *She* was real.

And very, very alive—

"What?" she said, and Ethan gave his head a sharp shake, then looked at her again.

"You want some coffee or something? Hot chocolate?"

She smiled, and things shifted a little more. "Coffee would be great, thanks."

* * *

By mid-December, between rehearsals and trying to prep holidazed kids for midterms, Claire was far too busy to dwell overmuch on that soul-baring convo the day after Thanksgiving. But occasionally—like after she'd fall into bed, too exhausted to monitor incoming thoughts, or when she'd see Ethan from a distance at school and he'd give her a friendly wave—it would occur to her that they'd untangled a lot more than light strings that afternoon.

Because… Okay, call her crazy, but she'd sensed an easing, she guessed she could call it, between them. An acceptance, maybe, of who they were and where they were coming from. Like, maybe…they were friends now?

In any case, in spite of the ever-present hum of holiday excitement, things felt calmer and more settled—for her, anyway—than they had in ages, she decided as she circled a big, red B+ on Roland's latest essay. And speak of the devil… She looked up at the kid's knock on her office door.

"Good timing," she said over the sound of the janitor running the big polishing machine in the hallway outside. "Just graded your paper." She held it out so he could see the grade, and his entire face lit up.

"Whaaa…?" he said, with a dig-me dip of the knees, then took it from her, the smile stretching as he scanned her comments. "I really did this?"

"You really did. Which I know since I watched you sit here and write it. I am so freaking proud of you, dude."

Rolling his eyes, he stuffed the paper in his backpack, then slung the bag over his shoulder again, one hand clamped around the strap. "You know what's really cool, Miss J? The way you tell us what we got *right,* too. Instead of, you know, only marking what's wrong."

Claire sat back in her chair, her arms crossed. "Well, of course. No sense in telling you what needs improvement if you don't know what's working."

"Yeah, that's what Coach says, too. Which is sorta why I'm here, actually. 'Cause I figured you should know." More beaming. "A scout from Michigan State was at the game on Friday."

The division championship game. Which Hoover had lost by one lousy point. But the team had played their hearts out, and Roland had made a last-second touchdown that—according to Juliette and Rosie—had been nothing short of a miracle.

Claire sucked in a breath. "And...?"

By now the kid's dreads were positively quivering with his excitement. "And...he stuck around to catch me after. Said we should talk more after the holidays, but he was interested. Real interested. Said I've got exactly the kind of talent they're looking for."

"Omigosh, Roland—" Claire got up to give the boy a high five "—that's wonderful!"

"Coach also said if there was one offer, there'd probably be others. Least, he said that's what happened with him. But...if it hadn't been for you kicking my butt about my grade in here—and then Coach's kicking it a second time to make sure I did whatever you said—none of this would be happening. So I just wanted to say thanks. Also, that I bought tickets for me and my folks to see the play. Because that seemed only fair."

Claire laughed. "Whatever works. But I'm so happy for you. You're earned this, Roland. So revel in it, okay?"

"You got it, teacher lady," he said, then left, fist-bumping the janitor on his way out. Goofball.

Doing a fair amount of grinning herself, Claire gathered up her things and slipped on her heavy coat. But instead of leaving the building through the door nearest her classroom, she trekked through miles of silent, dimly lit hallways to the other side, on the off chance that Ethan was still in his office.

He was, hunched over his desk with his chin in his hand and his forehead creased, a red pencil poised to attack the hapless page in front of him. Marking one of the state-mandated tests, no doubt, PE kids had to take these days and which Claire knew he hated with a purple passion. Smiling, Claire stood in the hallway, watching him, letting the wave of tenderness she felt for this quietly courageous man wash over her, and it occurred to her that in the infinite range of colors and tones that defined the ways we loved our fellow humans, admiration was definitely one of the brighter hues.

She rapped lightly on his door. Still frowning, he glanced up...and practically jumped to his feet. "Hey there! Uh...come on in—"

"No, that's okay, I need to get home, I promised my landlord I'd have dinner with him." At Ethan's curious expression, she laughed. "He's in his eighties. And gay. He also recently lost his partner," she said with a small smile. "So hanging out... I think it helps." He gave her one of those looks that sent her stomach into overdrive. "But anyway..." Her hand shook a little when she shoved her hair behind her ear. "Roland stopped by to tell me the great news."

The muscles eased in Ethan's brow. "Not sure which of us is happier about it, either. Although he couldn't have done it without you."

"Without both of us. Apparently it takes two to kick butt."

His chuckle sounded tired. "That one's butt, anyway." He slipped his hands into his pockets. "Guess we make a good team."

"Apparently so," Claire said, and the air thickened between them.

Ethan cleared his throat. "Actually, since you're here...

Jules's math tutor is leaving Hoover, so he's no longer an option. I was wondering if you knew of anybody else…?"

"Gosh, sorry… No. Not in math. But I'm sure the counseling office can help."

"Yeah, yeah, of course. Figured I'd check with you first, though. Since you seem to have a pulse on these things."

She humphed a short laugh. "I'm very flattered, but you're giving me way too much credit."

He smiled. "I'll let you go, then—"

"Um…yeah." She started to leave. "See ya 'round—"

"Oh, did Jules tell you?"

Claire turned back.

"She's sold every single thing she bought from that estate sale the two of you went to."

"No, she didn't. Good for her!"

"Yeah. Kid's got a knack. Good head for business."

Claire knew exactly where he was going with this, chose not to follow. "Clearly. Well. Give everyone my—" Love, she started to say. "Best. And have a good night. All of you."

"You, too," he said, his gaze locked in hers, and she thought, *Hell*.

Because, as she zipped out to her car, the thought nagged that despite what she'd wanted to see—to believe—about things easing between them… Had they really? If they'd truly settled into friendship—which was the only logical choice, given the circumstances—why had that conversation felt like a pair of shoes that didn't fit?

"Don't even bother answering that," she muttered to the universe.

Which was probably laughing its damn ass off.

The note from her counselor clutched in her hand, Juliette marched into the library during lunch on Friday, squinting slightly as she looked for her new tutor, some chick named Ashley Robertson. Man, she sure hoped this one was better than that other dude, who had the patience of a gnat. Him, she would not miss.

The library had set aside an area for tutoring alongside a bank of windows overlooking the courtyard. Juliette scanned the heads bent over books or sitting in corrals with headphones, her breath catching when she spotted Scott sitting at a far table by one of the windows.

"Stop it," she muttered to herself. "So he's in here, big fat deal…" And, oh, my *God,* what was he *doing?*

Standing, was what he was doing. And…waving her over?

What the hell?

She lifted the note—like he could see it from way over there, yeesh—and shook her head. But he gestured to her again. Nodding. And…smiling?

Juliette shook her head again, as if that would wake her up from what was obviously a dream. Then curiosity overcame horror and she made her way across the industrial carpet, clutching her math book so tightly to her chest she could barely breathe.

"I was looking for Ashley," she whispered.

"I know," Scott whispered back. "I traded students with her." Juliette blinked, not understanding. Scott grinned. "I'm your new tutor."

She nearly dropped the book. And her jaw. "How—?"

"Ash is better at algebra. Geometry's my baby. And…"

Holy cow, was he *blushing?*

"I figured helping you ace this class," he said, "was the best way to apologize for being a jerk to you. You didn't deserve that." At her continued gawking—because coherent speech was so not happening at the moment—he got even redder, then said, "I'm not a bad person, Julie. At least I'd like to think I'm not. But I sure acted like one, and I'm really, really sorry. Can you… Will you forgive me?"

Her eyes might have narrowed. One thing about coming from a large family? *Everybody* is all hot to warn you about boys who only want to play you. Rosie got the same thing—God knows they'd shared notes often enough. So it wasn't like she was naive or anything. In fact, she realized as her hammering heart slowed down enough to hear herself say, "Sure. Whatever," she was in total control of the situation.

Yes, even in the face of those adorable dimples when Scott grinned again, clearly relieved.

"Okay. That's…that's awesome. Thanks." She shrugged. Never mind how badly her knees were shaking. "So. Have a seat and let's get started. What chapter are you on?"

Nope, Juliette thought as she sat beside Scott and opened her book, trying like the dickens not to react to how good he smelled, *this time* she was not going to act like some lovesick chick. If this was fate… Fine. If not…

It was like Miss Jacobs said: if things were supposed to work out, they would. But you couldn't *force* them to. Meaning all she had to do—all she could do—was trust. With that thought, every bit of her nervousness dropped away. Okay, most of it.

And bonus points—her hair actually looked halfway decent for once.

So, bam.

Used to be, going to get the tree with four kids meant choosing one as quickly as possible before a) Jules got bored, b) Bella had to pee, or c) the twins wreaked havoc, got lost and/or drove innocent bystanders *up* the trees with their antics. This year, none of that seemed to be an issue—although Jules's dreamy grin was worrisome. Huh. However, three children's loudly delivered opinions about which tree was *the* tree—three, because Jules was clearly Not There—were meriting pretty much the same askance looks from other shoppers as in years past. Meaning he was doomed no matter what. And yes, every year he tried to talk the kids into a fake tree, and every year they looked so horrified he reneged. Not that he didn't understand—Merri had loved everything about the real tree, from the expedition to get the damn thing, to its "character"—meaning, how lopsided it was—to how it made the house smell like Christmas. Like *magic,* she'd said.

Yeah, whatever. She'd never had to drag the dead, dried-up thing out of the house every New Year's or vacuum up a gazillion dropped needles. There was nothing magic about messes, Ethan thought as they all finally settled on one that would at least fit in the house.

Of course, even he knew that his Grinch mood had far less to the do with the tree, or Christmas, or any of it, and far more to do with his confusion about a certain drama/English teacher whose smile and laughter and stupid, adorable curly hair had invaded the already overcrowded space in his head and refused to leave. Like the crush from hell. At thirty-eight. So wrong.

Then again, since he'd done things backward, anyway—falling in love at fifteen, a thought that made him totally sympathize with his and Merri's poor parents—it only made sense that he'd be doing the schoolboy infatuation thing now—

If that's what you want to call it, knucklehead...

Yeah, well, since that's all it could be...

Great. Now he was arguing with himself. *And the loony bin gets closer and closer,* he thought as he pulled into the driveway and his phone rang. He answered without bothering to check the display while the kids all piled out of the car and raced inside the house. Except for Number One Daughter, aka Miss Nosybody.

"Ethan? It's Sandy. I got your number off Mom's phone—"

Sandy. His half sister. God, when had he last seen her? Ten, twelve years ago—

"I know," she said, "it's been a long time, but—"

His heart stammering, Ethan got out of the car, motioning for Jules to follow. "Is Debbie okay?"

"Mom's fine. It's…it's my dad. He, uh, passed away a couple days ago. Heart attack."

Ethan leaned one hand on the car's roof, breathing in the pungent scent of fresh Noble fir. "Oh, Sandy… Damn." He'd been five when his birth mother remarried, had only met her husband once, when they'd come for his and Merri's wedding. But he'd liked him, was grateful to see how happy he'd made the woman who'd sacrificed so much. "You guys okay?"

"Dad was a ticking time bomb," his sister said on a sigh. "Overweight, hated to exercise, refused to quit smoking… Doesn't make it any easier, though. And Mom… She's kind of a wreck. The funeral's tomorrow. I doubt she'd expect you to come, I'm just going through her contacts list, calling everybody."

No, he didn't imagine any of them would expect his presence. Even so… "Look, text me the particulars.… I can't promise anything, with the kids and all. Or even if I can get a flight, but…I'll see what I can do. If you think it'd make any difference…"

Sandy punched out a breath. "You have no idea how much Mom talks about you and the kids. How she shows off the pictures you send, how proud she is of you. I mean, God knows she never thought you guys would stay close— in fact, she didn't want it, said it would've made things too complicated. But yeah—it'd make a difference." He heard a short, dry laugh. "Whether she'd admit it or not."

All too clearly, Ethan remembered how crucial the support of friends and family had been during those first horrible days after Merri's death, that he would have never gotten through her funeral without it. "I'll get back to you later," he said before disconnecting the call, then turned to find Jules giving him a quizzical look. He started working out the slipknots in the rope holding the netted tree on the roof. "My birth mother's husband passed away. I'm thinking… I think she'd appreciate it if I went out to the funeral. Which is tomorrow. Except everyone I'd ask to stay with you guys is either down with that crud going around or out of town."

"I don't understand—if you barely knew him, why would you go to his funeral?"

The tree freed, Ethan thunked it onto the driveway. "Not for him, for Debbie. Because…I can't even imagine the courage it takes to give your own kid up for adoption. Being there for her now… It's the least I can do for her. *If* I can figure out how to get there."

"Then you should totally go," Jules said, nodding. "I can take care of the other kids—"

"No way. *No,*" he said when his little warrior tried to protest. He hefted the tree and lugged it through the open front door generously setting free the heat from inside. "It's very sweet—and brave—of you to offer—" he shut the door, leaning the tree against the entryway wall and sending the dog into a sniffing frenzy "—but that's far too much responsibility for a kid. What if there was an emergency? You can't even drive yet."

"So I'd ask Rosie's mom—"

"Who has her hands full with her own kids. And I have no idea if I can even get a flight back tomorrow night—"

From the family room the twins sent up a roar. Ethan slanted a patient smile in their direction as Jules said, "How about Miss Jacobs?"

Ethan's head jerked toward his daughter. Then he laughed. "And here I thought you liked the woman."

"No, I'm serious. You've seen her with the boys. With

Bella. She'd be great. And no, I'm not trying to manipulate anything. I swear. But wouldn't she be a logical choice?"

"A few hours is very different from overnight. That's a huge imposition—"

"And I'll do all the cooking and make sure everybody gets their teeth brushed and stuff, I promise. She'd only be here as…backup. And the boys wouldn't be able to get anything past her, either."

This was true. But—

"Dad. If she doesn't want to do it, she'll say so. But if you don't ask, you'll never know." She dug his phone out of his jacket pocket, handed it to him. "So what've you got to lose?"

Only the last shred of dignity he still possessed, Ethan thought as he snatched his phone from his daughter and punched in Claire's number.

Chapter Nine

Claire was staring at the inside of her fridge, wondering if this was the night she'd finally starve to death, when her cell rang. Seeing Ethan's number in the display, her very empty stomach jumped.

"I need a huge favor" rumbled in her ear.

"Define huge."

"Like name your price, I'll pay it, huge."

The hair prickling on the back of her neck, Claire tucked one arm over her stomach. In the background, she heard the boys yelling, the dog barking, Bella whining about something. "Wow. Okay. What—?"

"One of my half sisters called a little bit ago. Dave, my birth mother's husband, passed away."

"Oh, Ethan, I'm so sorry—"

"Don't be. Not for me, I mean, I barely knew the guy. But for her... Yeah. I gather she's pretty torn up. The funeral's tomorrow, but no one else can stay with the kids while I'm gone. Everyone's either sick or away or already has kids or—"

"So you're asking me."

After a moment of silence, he said, "I'm sitting here staring at the Travelocity screen, ready to book a flight to Cleveland. But only if you say yes."

"Gee. No pressure or anything."

That got a weary laugh. "Debbie—my birth mother—has no idea I'm even considering coming. And my sister understands why I might not make it. But I'd really like to be there."

Claire shut her eyes. "Because you understand what she's going through."

Long pause. Then, "Pretty much, yeah. For whatever that's worth. Also, Jules says she'll do all the cooking and oversee the hygiene routine. Since asking you was her idea."

And that was *not* a pang of disappointment in the wake of his admission. Although knowing the request came from one of his kids actually made it a lot harder to say no. Which he undoubtedly knew. "So you need me to...?"

"Make sure the boys don't burn the house down, basically. And get bleeding children to the E.R., if necessary."

Claire looked at the cat, zonked out on his back in the middle of the sofa, totally oblivious to the fact that his mistress was desperately trying to fend off an impending panic attack. But what was she gonna say? No?

"Okay. Book your flight."

"You sure?"

"Ethan. Don't make me think too hard about this. Just do it."

"O...kay. Plane leaves from Philly at eight tomorrow morning, so I have to be at the airport by six, six-thirty, meaning I'll have to leave here by five at the latest—"

"Then that's when I'll be there."

"It's okay, Jules can hold the fort for a while. And they'll all be asleep—"

"I'll be there at five. Deal."

She heard a huge sigh of relief. "Funeral's at one, I'll book a return flight for later that evening. I should be back home by eleven or so."

"No hurry, we'll be fine."

"You do realize your voice is shaking, right?"

"It's, um, chilly in my apartment."

She heard a little "Heh-heh," then he said, "I cannot tell you how much—"

"For cripes' sake—enough, already. I'll see you tomorrow morning. Except for one thing."

"What's that?"

"There will be *no* bleeding. Understood?"

He laughed softly. "I'll make sure to pass along your instructions. And, Claire?"

"Yeah?"

"Thanks."

After he finally hung up, Claire plopped on the sofa beside Wally, earning her an upside-down, snaggle-toothed, one-eyed glare. Charming. "Oh, God, Wally…what have I gotten myself into?"

The cat yawned, stretched, then drifted back to sleep as if to say, *Yo, not my problem.*

Whoever came up with that thing about it being darkest before the dawn, Claire thought as she parked in front of Ethan's house the next morning, knew whereof he spoke. Dark, and damned cold. Shivering so hard her teeth rattled, she grabbed her purse and tote bag from the backseat, clutching her down coat closed as she scurried up the walk in her Crocs. Minuscule ice crystals assaulted her cheeks, making her flinch. Twenty percent chance of flurries, the Weather Channel said. Nothing to worry about.

Ethan opened the door before she reached it, bless his heart. For a moment, Claire frowned. He was dressed in a black suit and a camel overcoat, looking more like a corporate lawyer than a football coach. A seriously smokin' corporate lawyer—

"For the funeral," he whispered as he shut the door, and she nodded. Right.

Quit ogling, dummy.

Then, lowering his eyes to her penguin-dotted, fleece-lined pj bottoms, he smiled. "What on earth on you wearing?"

"Hey. Don't judge. They're warm."

The dog appeared, yawning and wagging his stubby little tail. Claire scooped him up to burrow her freezing face in his soft, warm fur and got little doggy kisses in return. She giggled, and now it was Ethan who was staring.

"Anyway," he said, "kids are still asleep. Bella usually gets up first, then Jules—she'll make breakfast—and you probably won't see the boys until noon. All the emergency numbers are on the blackboard in the kitchen, help yourself to anything in the fridge or whatever—"

"Dude. I've got this. Really."

"I know, I know. But…" He glanced up the staircase anyway, and Claire pushed out a breath.

"But you've never left the kids with a stranger," she said, and his eyes lowered to hers.

"You're hardly a stranger, Claire," he said with a small smile. "And if I didn't completely trust you, I would have never asked you to do this. Besides, I leave them with 'strangers' every day. Since I can't possibly vet everyone in the whole world. It's just—" another sigh "—I don't know why it feels harder now than it did at the beginning. But it does."

Claire cradled the dog more tightly to her chest to keep from touching the man standing so close she could smell his aftershave. "We'll be fine," she said. "I promise."

Ethan gave her one last, long look before, with a nod, he finally left the house.

Leaving Claire acutely aware that, until he returned, she was responsible for every living thing under its roof.

Holy crap.

Tangled up in a cozy throw on the family room sofa, the dog smushed behind her knees, Claire awoke with a start some time later. Thick, pewter-hued light flooded the evergreen-scented room, revealing a small, very bed-headed child standing on the other side of the coffee table, frowning at Claire as she hugged some unidentifiable stuffed toy to her chest.

"I'm sick," she croaked, and Claire sat up so fast the dog yelped.

"You are?" Claire said, her face scrunched, hoping like hell the kid would smile and say, *Just kidding, I'm fine.*

Instead, Bella gave her a solemn, bleary-eyed—or Claire may have been the bleary-eyed one, much too early to tell—nod. "My node id all 'tuffed up. And my throat hurts."

Somewhere in the middle of Claire's sleep-muddled brain, panic roared. Then reason wriggled past the panic, saying, *It's called a cold, Claire. Nobody's gonna die here.*

She tried a smile. "You want some juice? Or maybe some hot tea?"

"Juice," Bella said as a yawning, also bed-headed Juliette appeared in an outfit not dissimilar to Claire's, except with pups instead of penguins.

"Hey, Belly," she said, stretching. "What's up?"

"She's not feeling well." Claire pushed herself off the sofa and her feet back into her Crocs before heading toward the kitchen. "A cold, I think."

"Oh, yeah? Come here, baby," Juliette said, as Claire peered into the massive refrigerator. Which actually had stuff in it. Wow.

"Orange, apple or grape?"

"Apple," Bella said. Claire grabbed the bottle and closed the fridge door, looking over to see Juliette press her lips to the baby's forehead. Like Claire's mother used to do with her, she remembered. Like the girls' mother had probably done with them, she thought as her throat clogged.

"Yeah, probably. She's not warm or anything. Just miserable, huh?" the teen said, and Bella nodded. Juliette patted the sofa and Bella climbed on, smiling a little when her sister wrapped her up tight in the abandoned throw. Ever the opportunist, Barney jumped back up to wedge himself between the child and the back of the sofa. Yawning, her arms folded over her chest, the teen then padded over to the breakfast bar, shaking her head at the cup Claire had poured the juice into.

"She still spills a lot. In the cupboard by the fridge? There's cups with lids and straws. Yeah, those."

"Should I be doing anything else?" Claire asked, dutifully transferring the juice. "Like giving her cold medication or something?"

"Nah, we're pretty old-school around here. Liquids and rest, basically. As long as she doesn't have a fever, we're good." She smiled. "Jeez, you sound like you never had a cold before."

"And you sound like somebody's grandmother," Claire said, and the teen laughed, then sneezed. And sneezed again. She grabbed a tissue from a box on the bar, sneezed a third time, then looked at Claire.

"Crap," she said, and Claire thought, *Exactly*.

The good news was, the twins did not get sick. At least they hadn't by midafternoon. Nor did Bella get any worse, even if she seemed disinclined to move from the sofa, where she enjoyed an endless stream of mind-numbing kids' movies the rest of the day. The bad news was, however, that Juliette toppled like a felled tree and ended up crawling back into bed within an hour of getting up.

Leaving Claire—who finally got dressed right around when the boys emerged from their room in time for lunch—to play nurse/nanny/entertainment director for two sick kids and a pair of prepubescent boys who ate like wolves and were clearly at a loss without their video games. Because, of course, Bella had commandeered the TV. And practically snarled at any suggestion she share. Cute but fierce, that one.

None of which Claire shared with Ethan when he checked in around three. Man had enough on his mind, he didn't need to know that 50 percent of his progeny was sick—especially since it was clear their maladies were not in the least life threatening—or that the other 50 percent had taken bitching and moaning to a new level. Not to mention arguing with each other. Over nothing, as far as Claire could tell.

"I called Jules," he said, "but it went right to voice mail. She must've forgotten to charge her phone."

"Maybe so," Claire said, looking at the girl's phone where she'd left it before she'd done the zombie lurch upstairs and crashed.

"So everything's good? Kids all behaving?"

Upstairs, the boys started up again. Or still, since there really hadn't been much of a break that Claire could tell. "Of course, why wouldn't they be?"

His laugh sounded tired. "And did you think I couldn't hear that?"

"Criminy, you must have ears like a beagle."

"It comes in handy. So? Truth."

She sighed. "Okay, so the boys haven't shut up since they got out of bed, but I assume that's par for the course."

"I'm so sorry—"

"Don't be. I'm making them clean their room—"

"What?"

"Clean their room. Was I not supposed to do that?"

"Are they actually doing it?"

"I have no idea, I haven't checked. But they're quiet—okay, *quieter*—and I don't smell smoke, so I'm counting it as a win."

Ethan chuckled. "You fit right in," he said, and terror wrapped its nasty little paws around her neck and squeezed. Hard.

"So how's it going for you?" she asked, changing the subject.

"Me? I'm fine. Although I think Debbie is still in shock. She's got her kids and grandkids here, though, so that helps. She'll…she'll be okay. Not at first, maybe. But eventually."

Hearing the residual pain in his voice, Claire looked out the window. At the pretty, sparkly white *flurries* rapidly smothering the landscape. "How's the weather in Cleveland?"

"Messy," he sighed out. "Wet snow, sleet."

"Bad?"

"Enough to be taken seriously. How about there?"

"A few piddly flakes, off and on," she lied, thinking if she said it enough, she could make it so.

"Look, if I get stuck, you can call Dad, he'll be glad to come over—"

"No way would I ask him to drive in this—"
Damn.

"What happened to *piddly?*" he said.

"So maybe a little heavier than that. But we're all cozy and warm, and I see there's frozen pizza—"

"Pizza? Jules said she was going to make beef stew."

"Um…she had a paper to do or something, so we're going with pizza instead."

"Whatever works. Listen, feel free to crash wherever.

The sofa pulls out, but it's no great shakes. So use my bed, if you want—"

"Oh, no, I'm good with the couch. Hey, the boys need me, gotta go. And don't worry, okay? I've got it all under control, really."

Then she hung up before he could hear the tremor in her voice. And only partly from the prospect of being on call all night. Because now that Ethan had planted the idea of sleeping in his bed in her head...

Yeah, the sofa would do *just* fine.

"Miss Jacobs?" She looked up to see Harry and Finn in front of her. "Can Finn and me go over to the Valencias and play in the snow?"

Oh, God. She'd forgotten that, as the one in charge, she'd be the go-to person for stuff like this. That she'd have to actually make decisions that affected people she wasn't related to. True, she did that every school day with her students, but this was different—

Jeez, woman—snap out of it!

Claire tucked her chin to her chest and tried to look maternal. Or at least aunt...ernal. "Your room clean?"

Heads bounced. Vigorously.

"Really?"

"We can see the floor, does that count?"

She bit back a smile. "Beds?"

"Made."

"Clothes?"

The boys exchanged a glance. Busted. But Harry said, "Put away. Swear. Come look if you don't believe us."

So she tramped upstairs and did exactly that. And, indeed, the carpet was visible and the beds were made—after a fashion—and she could actually see the hamster cage. And the fish tank. And the other tank that held something...slithery. Shuddering slightly, her eyes cut to the closet. Behind her, the boys sucked in a collective breath.

Uh-huh. Intuition told her not to open the door. However, they had done what she'd asked with a minimum of groaning, and there was only an hour or so left of daylight, and if letting them go made her a big softie, so be it. So she said, "Just be back before it's fully dark, okay?"

They fled down the stairs, although Finn wheeled back long enough to give Claire a freckled grin and a thumbs-up, and, okay, she melted. Then she noticed, through Juliette's partially open door, the teen half sitting up.

"How're you doing?" she asked, pushing the door farther open.

"Better, actually." Juliette sniffed. "Not even stuffy. Weird." She squinted at the clock by her bed. "Was I really asleep that long?"

"You really were. Want anything?"

Juliette turned on her bedside lamp, then winced in the light. "Tea, maybe?"

"That, I can do. But why don't you take a hot shower first? Put on some clean jammies or sweats or something before you rejoin the land of the living?"

"That sounds awesome, yeah. Oh, shoot—I was going to make stew—"

"Don't worry about it, we'll have pizza."

"From Luigi's?"

"From DiGiorno. I seriously doubt Luigi's is delivering tonight." At the teen's frown, Claire said, "Look outside."

Draping herself in her brightly flowered comforter, the kid got up and padded over to her window "Wow. Oh, snap—can Dad even get back tonight?"

"Actually, I talked to him a few minutes ago, but he wasn't sure yet. So you might be stuck with me."

"Could be a lot worse. Wait…" Her head tilted. "Why is it so quiet?"

"Your brothers are out playing in the snow and your sister's asleep. Or she was when I came up here. So go take your shower, come downstairs whenever you're ready—"

"I'm so sorry for bailing on you—this wasn't how I saw things playing out it in my head."

"It's okay, sweetie—"

"But you're not used to this. My brothers—"

"Do not know the meaning of inside voices and are overly fond of body noises and have more energy than the sun. And yet, I survived."

Juliette softly snorted. "You sure?"

Leaning against the doorjamb, Claire crossed her arms. "I'm still here, aren't I?"

"By choice?"

She chuckled. "I'm here because your dad was obviously in a bind and I was only too glad to help. Especially since…since I'm guessing it takes a lot for him to ask for help."

"Boy, you got that right," Juliette muttered, and Claire smiled.

"Although he did tell me to call *his* dad if I got in over my head. And I'll admit there were a few times, especially early on, when I was tempted. Except then… I don't know. I got in the groove, I guess." She leaned forward and whispered, "And don't tell Finn, but he makes *awesome* fart noises."

Juliette giggled, then said, "Um, those probably weren't only noises."

Claire thought of the boys' roars of laughter after one particularly musical episode and grinned. "I was being… discreet. But what can I say? I like them. The boys, I mean. Not the noises." She paused. "I really like all of you."

The girl watched her for a second, then shuffled over to give Claire a hug, letting the comforter whoosh to the floor behind her. After a startled moment, Claire hugged her back, her eyes burning for the girl's loss. For everyone's.

"Sorry," Juliette mumbled, breaking away to wipe her eyes.

"No, it's okay—"

"Hey—could we make cookies later?"

Awkward moment over. Got it. "We?"

Juliette laughed. "Okay, *me*."

"Fine by me, but are you sure you're up to it?"

"Mom always said cookies make everything better."

"Can't argue with that," Claire said, then went downstairs, where the little one was stirring as well, yawning and hugging the...thing. And looking so blamed cute Claire could hardly catch her breath.

"Hey, pumpkin," she said, turning on a couple of lights in the darkening room. "Feeling better?"

Bella shrugged, swiped a shredded tissue across her red nose, then frowned at Claire. "That's what Daddy calls me."

Claire held out the trash can for the used tissue, handed over a clean one. "That's probably where I got it from, then—"

"Gotta pee," the child mumbled, then scrambled off the sofa and toddled off to the powder room. A minute later she toddled back, which was when Claire realized she was still in her pajamas, too. And barefoot.

"Need your slippers?" she asked, even as she thought, screw it about the pj's. Kid was six. And Claire sincerely doubted the queen was going to pop in.

Bella looked down at her feet, as though surprised to discover they were bare, then ran—good sign, Claire decided—upstairs, a minute later returning with puppies on her feet. By this time Claire had turned on several more lights and was in the kitchen, desperately trying to channel her inner domestic goddess, from whom she had not heard in years. If ever.

"Very cute," she said, nodding at the puppy slippers.

"Thank you." Bella climbed on a kitchen chair, tucking the slippers under her butt so she could sit on her knees, from which The Thing regally surveyed the goings on. "But they squish my toes. Could I have some more juice, please? Grape this time. If it's no bother."

Claire bit back her laugh. "Coming right up."

The kid chugged it all down, then released a very satisfied, and ridiculously adorable, sigh. And a burp. Then she said, "Thank you for taking such good care of me today," and Claire flushed to the roots of her hair.

"You're very welcome, sweetie." The microwave dinged.

"Whatcha making?"

"Tea. For your sister. Who, by the way, said she wanted to bake cookies after her shower."

Bella lit up. Then sneezed. "Christmas coo—" she sneezed again "—kies?" Claire nudged the box of tissues on the breakfast bar toward the child, who grunted a little trying to free one from its prison. "Like in shapes and stuff?" She blew her nose. After a fashion. "With lots of colors and sprinkles and those little red things?"

"Um...I have no idea.... Where are you going?" she asked when the little girl climbed down and marched out of the room, her companion clutched under her armpit.

She stopped in front of the dark, bare, definitely lonely looking evergreen standing in the corner. The boys had said they'd bought it the night before, but by the time Ethan had set it up it'd been too late to trim it. "The tree looks sad."

"It does, doesn't it?" Leaving the tea to steep, Claire joined Bella, crossing her arms. "Sad, and naked, and cold."

"Yeah," Bella said with a sharp nod. "It needs..." She waved her hand. "Lights. And stuff."

"Magic," Claire said.

"Yeah. Magic."

Claire looked down at her little charge. "I suppose we could, you know, decorate it. If you know where the ornaments are."

"Maybe in the garage? Jules knows. But..." More brow puckering. "But we always do that with Daddy."

"Well..." Claire squatted beside Bella to wrap an arm around her waist, resisting the urge to kiss the creamy little cheek. "We could either wait for Daddy, or we could all do it tonight after dinner, so it's all finished when he gets home." Claire thought of how tired Ethan sounded, how he'd had to cram this trip—and the emotional junk attendant thereto—into a life already full to the brim. "He might like that."

"I don't know..."

"How's about I ask him? Make sure it's okay?"

After a moment, Bella nodded. So Claire dug her phone out of her pocket and sent Ethan a short text: Bella wants to trim the tree tonight. OK by you?

Ten seconds later her phone dinged. God, yes.

Laughing, she started to pocket the phone when it dinged again. And bless you. For everything.

And heaven help her, she could *feel* Ethan's smile, that half-tilt of his lips that, until this very moment, Claire hadn't realized turned her inside out. Not *this* much, anyway. Longing shimmered through her, a tingling warmth that, under other, child-free, circumstances, might have provoked an actual gulp—

"Was that Daddy?"

Claire looked into Bella's sweet, impish face and felt another kind of tingling...another kind of longing. One she now realized she'd been denying for years, refusing to fall prey to the Self-Pity Monster she'd seen gobble up way too many other unmarried women over thirty.

"It was," she said over the monster's munching. "And

he said it's fine with him if we want to decorate the tree before he gets home."

"Cool," Bella said, bobbing her head. Then she suddenly wriggled around to frown into Claire's eyes. "You know, I think I like you."

Claire nearly choked on another swallowed laugh, as Juliette appeared in a clean set of pajamas, her damp hair in a million ringlets around her shoulders. A child after Claire's own heart. Or hair, in any case. "I like you, too, baby," she said, touching her forehead to Bella's. Then she turned to Juliette, on her way to the kitchen. "Your dad gave us the go-ahead to trim the tree. Bella says you know where the decorations are."

"In the closet under the stairs," Juliette said from kitchen. "We can get them out after dinner."

Succumbing to the irresistible pull of sweet little girl in her arms, Claire gave the top of Bella's head a quick kiss, then pushed herself to her feet to join her sister, stirring raw sugar into her tea.

"Jules? Something wrong?"

She shook her head, then twisted up her mouth. "The tree was Mom's thing," she said in a hushed voice. So Bella wouldn't hear, Claire presumed. Not that she could, since she was now playing tug-of-war with the dog and one of his toys. Between the growling and giggling, they were good. "Dad did all the decorating outside, Mom was in charge of inside the house—"

"Oh, sweetie, if you think I'm overstepping—"

"No! No, not all. In fact…" She pressed her lips together, her eyes glittering when she looked at Claire again. "Dad's tried so hard, you know? To keep things the same, making sure we still did all the stuff we used to with Mom. And maybe the others didn't notice, because they're younger, but I did, how much it was killing him. Mom…

She got as excited as a little kid about Christmas. And the tree was her favorite thing…."

Juliette swiped at a tear trickling down her cheek, and Claire's throat got tight. "So if I can't help thinking about Mom when we pull out her favorite ornaments, hang 'em on the tree…. I can only imagine how Dad feels." She gave Claire a watery smile. "Even though he acts all goofy and stuff so supposedly we won't notice."

Her own eyes burning, Claire leaned across the breakfast bar to wrap her hand around the girl's, giving her a smile. "Goofy? Your dad?"

"Amazing, but true. The only thing he won't do…"

When the teen stopped, Claire gave her hand a squeeze. "What?"

"Mom loved music. All kinds—classical, show music, rock, everything. And she listened to it *all* the time. There's a ton of her CDs still in her office, Dad never got rid of them…but he never plays them, either."

"Maybe he's not a music person?"

Juliette shook her head. "He'd play it plenty when Mom wasn't around. But since she died he won't listen to music at all. Any music. Isn't that sad?"

Squeezing Juliette's hand again, Claire went around to pull the pizzas out of the freezer, her own memories pinching her heart. "Sounds familiar. Both my parents adored opera, but after my father died my mother said it hurt too much to hear it, because she associated it so strongly with him. So I don't think what your dad's feeling is all that unusual."

Juliette straddled one of the chairs at the kitchen table, her hair tumbling over her shoulders. "So your mom never listened to opera again?"

"I think she tried to once or twice. But after that… No. Not really."

A huge sigh pushed from the girl's lungs. "It's like…

they're broken." Her eyes widened. "Is that what death does? Breaks people?"

"It can," Claire said honestly. "*If* they let it. If *you* let it. Do you feel broken?"

After a moment, Juliette wagged her head. "Changed, maybe. And still sad. But not like I'll never feel whole again."

"Then I think you're good." They heard more giggling, then barking, as Bella and Barney raced up the stairs. Claire smiled. "To be honest, after my father died, I sometimes got the feeling Mom was only biding her time until she could join him. And that *is* sad. On the other hand, there's my landlord—he and his partner had worked and lived together for more than fifty years until Thomas died last year. But even though you can still hear the affection in Virgil's voice when he talks about him, he says he's got a list as long as his arm of things he still wants to do. That why should his journey come to a halt because Thomas is continuing his somewhere else?"

Juliette's brow crunched for a moment before she slowly nodded. "I like that."

Claire smiled. "Me, too." The pizzas set on two cookie sheets, she slid them into the oven. "Some people give up, some go on. Just depends."

"Which do you think my dad is?"

The oven door closed, Claire turned. "You know him a lot better than I do. What do *you* think?"

Another frown preceded, "Hard to tell. Somewhere in the middle, maybe?"

"Nothing wrong with that. Because he's doing what's right for *him*. And he's obviously doing right by you guys, far as I can tell. Or am I off base about that?"

The corners of the girl's mouth curved up. "No. You're not. He's a great dad. Even if he won't let me date until I'm sixteen."

"Which, actually, is part of what makes him a great dad, no?"

Juliette rolled her eyes right as the twins exploded through the back door into the mudroom, both talking a mile a minute as they shucked off their wet clothes and—Claire saw—dumped them in heaps on the tiled floor.

"Hey," she said, doing the turn-right-back-around thing with her index finger when they came galumphing into the kitchen. "Ain't nobody here gonna clean up after you, so hang up your stuff. Got it?"

Julie and the twins exchanged a three-way glance.

"What?" Claire said, which got a trio of shrugs.

"Nothin'," Finn said, a moment before he and Harry trooped back to the mudroom to scoop their crap off the floor and sling it over the many hooks provided for exactly that purpose. But Claire caught the grins, oh, yes, she did.

And damned if she didn't feel...triumphant.

Chapter Ten

Snow smothered the town like a thick down comforter, pale gold in the early-morning sun. Ethan parked the Explorer in the drive, then stealthily let himself inside, grabbing the excited dog before he could start barking.

"Yeah, yeah, I'm back," he whispered, muffling his own chuckles as Barney slathered Ethan's whiskery face in sloppy kisses. Except for the steady ticking of the grandmother clock in the crook of the stairs and the overcaffeinated beating of his own heart, silence cushioned the still-cold house. Out of the corner of his eye, he caught a flash of sunlight bouncing off the decorated tree in the living room's bay window. Still holding the dog, Ethan came closer, his lips pressed together to stifle a laugh. Judging from the helter-skelter placement of the ornaments—not to the mention that most of them were crowded on the lower branches—he guessed that Claire had let the kids trim the tree without her interference. That, or tree trimming was not one of her talents....

Speaking of whom… He glanced at the sofa to see some rumpled blankets, one of Jules's pillows, but no Claire. Not that he'd blame her for eventually choosing his bed over the sucky couch—and from those nights when he'd had a cold and didn't want to disturb Merri, he knew the pathetically thin pullout mattress wasn't any better—but now he had an image of Claire in his bed, her curls all tangled, making his sheets smell like her…

Man, those five-hour energy drinks were *wicked*.

He finally set down the dog and shrugged off his topcoat, wanting nothing more than to get out of this suit and into his jeans and a sweatshirt. But that meant going to his room. Maybe if he was really quiet…

The dog practically tripping him, Ethan crept up the stairs and past the boys' room—both kids were sprawled across their beds at crazy angles, no covers, all appendages accounted for—then Juliette's closed door, before reaching the master bedroom. Where the door stood wide-open. Cautiously, he peeked into…an empty room. Bed still made, no girl stuff strewn about—

Ethan's chin jerked down when he felt a tug on his pants leg—Barney, clamped on and determined that Ethan follow him. For a moment he freaked—wasn't that what dogs did when somebody was in trouble?—until he realized if that'd been the case the dog would've gone ballistic the moment Ethan walked through the door. "What is it, boy?"

The dog immediately let go and pranced the few feet to Bella's room, where he sat and—Ethan could have sworn—cocked his head toward the door.

Obediently he looked inside…and dissolved. Because there they were, his baby girl snuggled against Claire's chest, Bella's poufy, pastel quilt loosely drawn over the pair of them. A half dozen storybooks lay scattered on the quilt, the floor; on the nightstand, the bedside lamp—a teddy bear in a tutu that Merri had gotten her when she turned three—still glowed.

As did the pair of them, Bella's silky blond strands entwined with Claire's curls, Claire's left arm cradling his baby's shoulder as they breathed in sync.

He couldn't move. Hell, he could barely breathe. The sweetness punched his barely healed heart, making his eyes burn, even as guilt slammed through him at what he'd been imagining before, even if only briefly. Before he could duck away, though, Claire stirred, her eyes drifting open. She started, her hand going to her mouth to block her gasp. Then she smiled, a sleepy, beautiful smile that delivered a second punch far worse than the first.

"Busted," she said soundlessly, then inched away from the sleeping little girl, clumsily extracting herself from the quilt to get to her feet. She was wearing jeans, he saw, along with a soft-looking sweatshirt the color of raspberry ice cream. Her curls slithered over her shoulders when she quickly bent to grab those god-awful rubber shoes of hers, then silently crossed the floral rug and through the door to Ethan, now standing in the hall.

"She woke in the middle of the night," she whispered. "So I thought reading a few books would ease her back to sleep. Guess it worked for both of us." She blinked up at him. "When did you get in?"

"Five minutes ago," he said, trying not to notice her flushed cheeks, her wild hair. The lingering scent of perfume on her sleep-warmed skin. *Really* trying not to notice the effect all of it was having on him. Never mind that guilt was still all up in his face like some smart-assed street kid, going, *Yo, remember me?*

Remember your wife?

Except yearning's whisper was far more importunate. And dangerous.

"The snow had stopped," he said, forcing himself not to look away, to face this thing down and prove his dominion over it, "but everything was so backed up I wouldn't have been able to get out until later this morning. So I rented a car. Got the last one on the lot."

Wide-eyed, Claire folded her arms over her stomach. "You drove all night? In the *snow?*"

Ethan smiled. "It was clear by then. And I-76 was good." He curled his palm around the back of his stiff neck as his gaze landed once more on his sleeping daughter. "It was making me crazy, being away. Being stuck. I had to get back, one way or the other. Would've been here sooner, but had to drop the car off at the airport, pick mine up—"

"Hey." When his eyes met hers again, he saw the faintest trace of annoyance, even though her lips tilted. "We were fine."

Sheer exhaustion, combined with relief at being home again—those were the only reasons he could think of to explain the ache of desire, deep in his gut. The nearly overwhelming compulsion to cup her jaw, simply...to touch. To *feel*...

Ethan tried to smile, but it felt a little wonky. "I know you were. I wasn't..." His cheeks puffed out with the force of his expelled breath. "I wasn't worried. I just wanted to be home."

Her eyes softened. "Of course you did," she said, laying a hand on his upper arm, gently chafing it for a moment before another yawn attacked.

"Sorry," she said, covering her mouth with the back of her hand. "Need coffee. Also, potty."

"And I need to change before this suit becomes one with my skin."

"There's a lovely image," she said with a low, gravelly, still-sleepy laugh. "So go change. I'll meet you in the kitchen."

* * *

Claire got a load of herself in the bathroom mirror, gri-maced, shrugged and followed the scent of coffee down-stairs to find Ethan standing in front of the tree with his hands jammed into the back pockets of his jeans and a lopsided grin on his still-unshaved face.

"We were all a little slaphappy by the time we finished," she said, heading for the kitchen and the magic elixir beck-oning to her from same. "I had no idea it took so long to decorate a tree. At least one this size." She found a mug, poured her coffee. "We always had this puny little fake thing when I was a kid." The mug cradled in her hands, she joined Ethan. "And Mom always did it on Christmas Eve anyway, so it'd be there like some big surprise when I woke up."

"What about when you lived in New York?"

"Sometimes the roomies got a tree, sometimes not. Since I never really bonded with any of them, I didn't bother." She took another magnificent sip, reveling in the steam on her face as much as the very welcome jolt to her system. "And now that I live alone, I'm back to the little fake jobber. So decorating that one," she said, nodding toward the tree, "was fun. Actually..." Another sip dis-patched, she said, very carefully, "Being with the kids... I enjoyed it." Her lips curved. "Mostly."

She sensed his gaze swing to her profile, then back to the tree. Heard his quiet chuckle. "Sounds about par for the course. And anybody who tries to tell you that life with kids is always fun is full of it. Hey, pumpkin..." Setting his coffee on a nearby table, Ethan squatted as a sleepy Bella padded into the room, then ran to him. "Miss me?" he said, tucking her against his chest.

The little girl rubbed her cheek against her father's shoulder, then sniffed. Loudly. And sneezed. Ethan im-mediately set her apart, frowning. "You okay, baby?"

"She has a little cold," Claire said. "No biggie."

"Jules, too," Bella said, and, sure enough, Ethan's head snapped up so Claire could get the full effect of his frown.

"*Colds,* Ethan. Not the plague."

"The boys...?"

"Are fine. But then, I'm beginning to think they're alien life forms anyway, impervious to things like viruses and germs and such. So no surprise there."

At that, the frown eased, replaced by a short laugh. "You may have a point." He got to his feet, hauling the baby up with him, and the love in his eyes when he looked at his daughter... Oh, dear God. "But you still should have told me."

"And what would you have done about it?" Claire said gently over a microspurt of annoyance. "Because we were totally good, weren't we, sweetie?" she said to Bella, who gave a vigorous nod.

"*Totally* good," the baby echoed, then sniffed. Balancing her on his hip, Ethan swooped to snatch a tissue from a box on the coffee table, then righted them both again, expertly folding the tissue over the tiny nose.

"Blow," he ordered, and she did. Kind of. Then he looked at Claire. "And I would have wanted to know for *your* sake. Okay, theirs, too, but mostly for you. Because I know this is totally outside your comfort zone, and I might've been able to help more than you think. Yes, from several hundred miles away. Bad enough I asked you to watch them for an entire day—at the last minute, no less—but to foist sick kids off on you, as well—"

"Which they weren't when you left. So you can stop with the mea culpa routine, jeez."

Ethan's brows lifted, humor glittering in his eyes and tugging at his mouth, and Claire's sleep-slogged brain joined forces with her pitifully deprived girl parts to conspire against her, sending up a steady tattoo of *want, want, want* through her veins.

Like, *really* loudly.

Turning smartly on her heel, she retreated to the kitchen to rinse out her now empty mug and set it on the drain board, almost painfully aware that Ethan was watching her every move. She half wondered what he was thinking, decided she didn't want to know. Since whatever it was, it couldn't possibly bode well. For either of them.

"Well," she said, returning to the living room to retrieve her coat and purse and tote bag from where she'd dumped them on a chair the day before. "I guess my work here is done, so I'll be off—"

"We could all go out to breakfast," Ethan said, which got an enthusiastic nod from Bella and, probably, a bug-eyed gawk from Claire. "Because," he said, all intense blue eyes, "the least I can do is feed you. To say thank you?"

Well, of course. Totally reasonable. Except... "Everyone else is asleep?"

"I'll go wake them up!" the little girl said, wriggling out of her father's arms and racing up the stairs, yelling, "Hey! Boys! Get up!" at the top of her lungs.

"Not for long," Ethan said, his mouth hitched into a ridiculously sexy smile. Although Claire sincerely doubted that was his intention. Which was made it so sexy. Not to mention ridiculous. Dammit.

And which made her need to *get the hell out of there* all the more pressing. Years, it had taken her, to finally, fully catch on to the concept of self-respect. Not to mention emotional self-preservation. So damned if she was about to let a sexy smile derail her. Even if that smile came as part of a package that included humor, tenderness and a protective nature that made her ovaries spin like Tasmanian devils.

"Um...thanks, but...I have stuff to do and...stuff. So I really need to go—"

"You're not going to breakfast with us?" Bella—who'd reappeared like a genie—asked, her forehead all crumpled. Claire squatted and the little girl moved right into her arms. Of course.

"Not this time, baby," she said, pushing past the knot in her throat even as she clung to the last remaining shreds of her common sense by the very tippy-tips of her fingernails. She reared back, smiling, wondering where the woman who didn't think she wanted kids had got off to and who the hell this chick was she'd left in her place. She tapped Bella's nose. "But I'll see you at Juliette's play, right?"

"When's that?"

"Friday night. Right before Christmas vacation starts." She glanced up at Ethan, who was looking at her with that same expression she'd caught when she'd first woken up. Except then she'd thought she'd only imagined it, what with her still being half-asleep and all. Apparently not. "You are coming, right?"

"Of course," he said, with a "what are you, nuts?" dip to his brows.

Claire looked back at Bella, who was toying with one of Claire's curls, a sweet gesture that twisted her heart even more. "So I'll see you then?"

The child nodded, then linked her arms around Claire's neck and pulled her close, and now Claire thought her heart would incinerate. "I love you," Bella whispered, then kissed Claire's cheek before running up the stairs again.

Blushing, Claire got to her feet, swaying slightly for a moment before finally working up the courage to look at Ethan again. But either he hadn't heard Bella's declaration or was ignoring it or—option three—the kid gave her heart to everybody so this was no big deal. In any case, all he did was walk Claire to the front door and open it, flooding the entryway with bright white light.

"Well. Thanks again."

Claire nodded, opened her mouth, realized she had absolutely no idea what to say and walked out into the crisp, beautiful morning a helluva lot more conflicted than she had been when she'd arrived the day before.

There'd been no way, of course, Ethan would've told Claire that Bella hadn't shown that kind of affection to anyone other than family since her mother's death. Bad enough that Jules—clearly on a high after her performance and talking nonstop to her grandparents in the packed Performing Arts Center's lobby—had yet to let a day pass without singing Claire's praises. Effusively. About how she hadn't even flinched when she'd realized Jules and Bella were both sick, or taken any guff from the boys, or even tried to influence the kids' tree-decorating decisions.

Yep, a born salesperson, that one.

Not that any hard sell was needed, although Ethan wasn't about to share that bit of information, either. With Jules or anyone else. Bad enough that nearly a week later, he still hadn't gotten over his reaction to Claire that morning— a reaction only reprised every time he saw her at school. Or, like now, as he heard her distinctive laugh, caught a glimpse of her shiny curls as she worked the crowd. So, yeah—he was smitten. And *hell,* yeah, tempted...despite the laughable impracticalities of even trying to see where that temptation might lead.

And hallelujah for impracticalities, he thought as she finally made her way through the throng to them, her smile bright—she was wearing lipstick, he noticed, a bright red that actually made his mouth go dry—her joy a palpable thing, radiating more brightly than the Christmas lights on Main Street. Ethan had never seen her dressed in anything but her weird outfits, so her simple black dress, dark stockings and pumps—even if those were the same color as her lipstick—came as a shock. As did the way the clingy fabric hugged her curves, the neckline dipping just low enough to hint at cleavage…peeking out from underneath a necklace of blue and green stones roughly the size of the Christmas wreath on his door. It was all so…Claire, he thought with a smile.

As the twins shyly grinned, looking almost civilized in the sweaters and khakis Ethan had insisted they wear, Jules squealed and gave her teacher a hug, then introduced her to Merri's parents. Claire's eyes softened as she took one of Carmela's hands in both of hers before wordlessly pulling the plump, dark-haired woman into a hug. He could count on one hand the number of women he knew who expressed that kind of selflessness, two of whom were right in front of him.

And the other two—Jeanne and Merri—were gone.

Dulled though it may have been, pain streaked through him, along with the same warning that had played in his head with both increasing frequency and urgency the past several days:

Do not go there.

Do not set yourself up for more hurt, more misery… more hell—

"Dad? You okay?"

Ethan snapped back to attention to smile for his daughter, avoiding Claire's curious glance as she talked with both grandfathers. "Sure, honey. I'm fine."

"I was just remarking," Carmela put in, "about how impressed we all were with her performance. I had no idea Julie was so talented. Best Ghost of Christmas Past I've ever seen!"

"Isn't she?" Claire said, her gaze deliberately bouncing off Ethan's before returning to Carmela's, then John's. She laughed. "And I'm not only saying that to blow up you guyses' skirts." Slipping her arm around Jules's waist, she gave his daughter a quick squeeze. "She's a real natural."

"Yes, she is," Ethan agreed, taking a perverse pleasure in seeing his daughter's gasp of surprise. Of course, she had no idea about his standing outside her room the night before, hearing her go over her lines with Rosie, the almost electric shock that had gone through him when he'd realized her gift.

And to deny her the opportunity to see where that gift took her, no matter the risk, would only make him a jerk of the first order.

Behind her, Claire's eyes went shiny as she pressed her hand to her chest, giving him a short, slight nod before resuming her conversation with the grandparents, while the twins took Bella over to the refreshment table. Jules, however, let the crowd wash around her as she faced Ethan, arms crossed, brow puckered.

"Did you mean it?"

"Hey. Did you notice how still the audience got, like they were hanging on your every word?"

Her mouth twisted to one side. "I was kinda busy up there."

"Well, they did. And if this is something you really want to pursue, I won't stand in your way. Because what I saw tonight..." He shook his head, as if that would dislodge the lump in his throat. "It was magic, is the only word for it. And your mother would be... What was that expression she liked to use? Over the moon, that's it. I couldn't be prouder, honey."

"Oh, Daddy..." Juliette's eyes glittered before her arms wrapped around his waist. But the moment was short-lived when that Scott person appeared, looking sheepish and determined at the same time. Jules had finally confessed that, yes, her new tutor was indeed the boy in the cast she'd let upset her at the mall on Black Friday, but that she was completely over it now. Judging from the startled look on his daughter's face, he somehow doubted it. Judging from the look on the *boy's* face—he had waited until Ethan let his daughter go before extending his hand—Ethan seriously considered adding a forty-foot tower to the house.

"Nice to see you, Coach Noble," the boy said with a firm, confident shake. Point to him. "Scott Jenkins—"

"Yes, I know who you are. Jules tells me you've been a huge help with her math."

The kid turned his smile on Jules, whose glittery grin was only surpassed by the boy's. And he wasn't even wearing braces. "Can't take a whole lot of credit for that. Julie's ridiculously smart—"

"I've always thought so," Ethan said. Sternly.

"I know, right? But between you and me, Mr. Noble..." Scott leaned in to Ethan, his voice lowered as his eyes darted furtively around the noisy lobby. "Miss Henry is nice and all, but she isn't the greatest at explaining things. So it was really only a matter of finding another angle."

His grin at his own joke seemed slightly nervous. Good. "As it were. Once I did that, Julie immediately caught on. Anyway..." He straightened. "My parents—they're over there—" he pointed to a reasonable enough–looking middle-aged couple a few feet away "—are hosting the cast party at our house. So I was wondering if it'd be okay with you if I took Julie? Not as a date," he hurriedly added, "because she told me you won't let her date until she's sixteen, but...as a friend?"

Brows raised, Ethan looked at his daughter, who was staring at the boy openmouthed. Beside him, Scott prattled on.

"I mean, we don't live very far, and you can talk to my parents, if you like. But I can promise you, sir, there won't be any alcohol or drugs or anything like that. And Miss Jacobs'll be there, too. And she's worse than my parents. About making everybody toe the line," he said, his face turning more red than Juliette's.

That was definitely true, Ethan thought, remembering what Jules had said about Claire's interaction with the pair of monkeys currently masquerading as his sons. He also recalled his own pleas to Carmela and John, all those years ago, to let him go out with their daughter, the anxiety in their eyes even as they finally, reluctantly, said okay when they were sixteen. The combination of guilt and excitement as holding hands led to sweet kisses, which quickly escalated into heated kisses, which in turn naturally and inevitably led to all those things every parent fears and no parent wants to think about. Not when they were sixteen, no, but by eighteen…

A cold chill streaked up Ethan's spine.

But right now, they were only talking about a chaperoned cast party at somebody's house. And Claire would be there. He could count on her.

Without a shred of doubt.

"Let me talk to your parents."

Scott nodded, his Adam's apple bobbing. "Sure thing…"

So he did, and got his reassurances, and then Claire appeared to tell him she'd have Jules home by midnight, and he got another hit of her perfume and his brain tripped for a second. Then he watched his baby walk off with some hormone-addled teenage boy with Claire beside them, that dress cupping her ass, swaying slightly as she walked in those killer red heels.

And he closed his eyes, swearing.

Oh, dear, Claire thought as she pulled into Ethan's driveway and caught a glimpse of Juliette beside her, her expression so rapturous in the glow from the Christmas lights Ethan hadn't yet turned off that a casual bystander might think the girl'd had an angel visitation.

"Um…you're home?"

"I know." Juliette sighed, slowly unbuckling her seat belt. "Was that the best party ever, or what?"

"It was very nice," Claire agreed, unlatching her own belt, and Juliette frowned.

"You don't have to see me inside, you know."

"Have you *met* your father?" she said, the precise moment Ethan opened the front door.

The teen sighed again, then shrugged. As though not even the world's most protective daddy was going to mar this most perfect of nights.

"You said midnight," the daddy in question muttered as Juliette floated past him.

"For pity's sake, it's five after—"

"Ten after."

Claire ignored him. Well, as much as one could ignore the presence of this hubba-hubba hunk taking up his entire front door opening. "And Scott's mom is not someone to whom you simply say, 'I had a great time, thanks so much,' and leave. Man, can that woman talk—"

"So...everything was on the up-and-up?"

"Aside from the kegs set up in the dining room? Sure thing. For God's sake, Ethan," she said, laughing when the frown deepened. "I'm kidding. And you are way too much fun to tease."

"Sorry. It's just..."

"She's your baby girl, got it. And if it makes you feel any better, I did not let her out of my sight for a second. Not that she knew that, of course. Swearsies," she said, and he finally blew out a breath. Maybe even smiled.

"Thank you," he murmured, his gaze locked in hers, and, oh, dear *God,* did she ache to skim her fingers over that tight jaw, those shoulders so tense with responsibility.

"You're very welcome. Well—"

"Um...you want to come inside...?"

And heaven help her, she actually hesitated. "No, it's

late. And I'm about to crash. But…you guys gonna be around tomorrow? I've got some presents for the kids."

There went the frown. "You didn't have to—"

"Know that. Not the point. So…I'll swing by tomorrow afternoon?"

"Uh…yeah. Sure. I think their grandparents are taking them shopping tomorrow morning, but they should be back by two or so?"

"Then I'll be by sometime after that," she said, then turned to go.

"Claire?"

Halfway to her car, she swiveled back. "Yeah?"

"Text me when you get home. Let me know you got there okay."

She couldn't help the laugh. Or the thump in the pit of her stomach. Since when did he care whether she got home safely? Since when did anybody? "I'm a big girl, Ethan."

"And it's late, and the roads look like they might be getting icy. So humor me, okay?"

"Fine, fine," Claire said, giving him a backward wave as she returned to her car. Where she and her still-thumping stomach sat behind the wheel for a moment, trying to decide whether that sound in her head was more *aww*…or *argh!*

Either way, she thought as she put her car in Reverse and backed into the street, it was freaking her the hell out.

Like, seriously, dude.

Chapter Eleven

If the dog hadn't gone into his frenzied barking routine late the next afternoon, Ethan—in the office wrapping presents—would've never realized the doorbell had rung. Or—when he opened the door to find Claire with a shopping bag brimming with Santafied goodies—that he'd completely spaced about her coming over.

"You look surprised," she said, amusement dancing in her eyes as she removed her sunglasses, then rammed the earpieces into her curls, and Ethan felt he'd been sucker punched. In, oh, so many ways. For, oh, so many, *many* reasons.

"I'm—" he blew out a breath "—an idiot. Please…come in. The kids aren't here, though," he said behind her as she did, and he caught a whiff of that damned perfume, tangled up with the crisp scent of the cold, and more sucker punching ensued. Also, stirrings. Of the damn-it-all-to-hell kind.

"Oh?" She turned, setting down the bag on a bench by the door, then facing him again, fidgeting with her long scarf. Bright purple. Fuzzy. Soft. Probably smelled like her perfume. "Not home yet?"

He forced his eyes to her face. Crossed his arms over the rattiest sweatshirt he owned. Wondering how he'd forgotten about her when he'd barely slept for thinking of her all damn night. "Not coming home. Tonight, I mean. Which is why I'm an idiot, because if I'd remembered, I would've called you. Their grandparents decided to take them into the city to see the show at Radio City, do the whole Christmas in New York thing. Stay overnight at the Plaza—"

"Wow." She pressed her lips together. No lipstick, he noticed. This was not a turnoff. "They got rooms at the last minute like that?"

"No, they'd apparently had it planned for months, but didn't tell me because they didn't trust me not to let it slip to the kids."

Her eyes twinkled. "Bad at keeping secrets, are you?"

"Notoriously so. So I didn't know any of this until they picked the kids up this morning. And then I thought of the five million things I could get done without them here, and…" He felt his face warm. "I totally forgot about you. Not about *you*," he said when she laughed. Then he puffed out a breath. "You know what I mean."

"And I even texted you last night."

Yeah. A single word: Home.

Of course, his response had been equally succinct: OK.

"I know. Like I said. Idiot."

"So…" She looked around. "You're all by yourself?"

"Just me and the beast." Who'd planted his fuzzy butt on the toe of Ethan's sneaker. Smiling, Claire glanced at the dog, then back at Ethan, and the ramifications of their being alone slammed into him, knocking all those years of being a responsible adult clear into next week. Especially when she said, "Wow. You could do anything you want, huh? Anything at all."

"I know. The freedom… It's heady," he said, and she snorted a light laugh. "So I've been wrapping presents. Speaking of which… You can put yours under the tree, if you want."

"Okay. Sure," she said, picking up the bag again and walking into the living room, slowly unwrapping the scarf with one hand. Then she stuffed a curl behind her ear, dislodging the sunglasses, which she caught before they got past her shoulder. She was only wearing the tiny diamond studs today, more flash than substance. The exact opposite, he mused, of the woman wearing them. "Wow. I see they've been working on it."

"Not *they*. Jules. A trait she inherited from her mother," Ethan said, watching Claire as she carefully set the packages among the others. From the hall behind them, the grandmother clock chimed. One…two…three…four… "The tree was never really done, as far as she was concerned. She'd keep adding things, moving stuff around… even after Christmas." He pushed out a quiet laugh. "It was nuts."

Standing again, Claire gave him much the same look he'd seen her give Merri's parents the night before. In that situation, it had worked. Now, for some unknown reason, it irked the hell out of him. "She sounds—"

"Don't you dare say perfect."

"I was going to say…fun."

"Okay, yeah. In her own way."

Chuckling, she came closer, the sunglasses hooked into the front of her vest. God, he hated that vest. Almost more than those hideous patterned leggings. And the clunky boots.

"What does that mean?"

"Mer wasn't crazy fun—" *Like you are,* Ethan almost said. "Not…roller-coaster, jack-in-the-box fun. But she enjoyed the little things, you know? She made ordinary things special. Like baking cookies." His gaze returned to the tree. "Decorating Christmas trees."

"And you'll always miss her."

The kindness lacing her words sliced right through him. So much so it took a moment to get out the simple "Yeah." At her silence, he cupped the back of his neck. "Everybody keeps telling me I need to get over it."

"Right. Like you're just supposed to forget someone you loved for more than twenty years? What a load of B.S."

Ethan almost smiled. "The pain, I think they mean. Not her." He paused, then said, "Jules was telling me about your mother, how she never really got past your father's death?"

"Not really, no," she said, and sighed. "I don't mean she did a Miss Havisham or anything, getting stuck in a time warp after he died. She functioned. Kept up with what was going on in the world. But she wasn't any too keen to stick around, either. In some ways I think she almost welcomed her illness."

Ethan looked back at the tree. "That's so sad."

"You would think. Except she honestly believed she'd accomplished everything she needed to here, so why stay? And it certainly wasn't my place to convince her otherwise." She looked over at him, a tiny smile on her lips. "It's nobody's business how anyone else handles their grief. Especially when they haven't been in the other person's shoes."

Ethan felt something knock in his chest. "Too bad more people don't share your philosophy."

"I've always thought so," she said, smiling as Barney picked that moment to abandon his spot on Ethan's sneaker and shuffle over to sniff Claire's boot. Squatting to pet him, she laughed when he flopped on his back so she'd rub his belly.

"Damn dog has no shame," Ethan muttered, wondering why she was still there, wondering why he was glad she was, as Claire chuckled again. Then Ethan heard himself say, "You looked good last night," and her head jerked up. "In that dress. And that thing," he said, indicating his neck.

"Necklace?"

"Yeah. Necklace. And those shoes."

Another laugh. "What on earth brought that on?"

"No idea." He rammed his fingers into his jeans' pockets, remembering. "But you should dress like that more often."

"Like a grown-up, you mean?"

"Like…a woman."

"Is there a compliment in there somewhere?"

"I said you looked good, didn't I? And if that sounded sexist, I'm sorry—"

Grinning, she got to her feet. "It does, a little. Except I know you didn't really mean it that way. So thank you." She paused, then said, "I only have two dresses. Both black. One for winter, one for summer—"

"I should hook you up with my sister."

"Pardon?"

"Sabrina. She works with fashion. In New York."

"I think that's called digging yourself in deeper."

"Yeah, I'm good at that." As if she were magnetized, Ethan came closer, fingering the edge of her scarf. To keep from touching her hair. Her cheek. "See this color? It looks real good on you."

Silence thrummed between them for a long moment before his eyes lifted to her face, where he saw her pupils dilate, her lips slightly part, her pulse hammer at the base of her neck.

"It looks better off," Claire said, her voice barely above a whisper. He yanked his hand away.

"What?"

She lowered her eyes for a moment, then lifted them to his, her cheeks ruddier than usual. "I didn't come over here to seduce you. Obviously. Since for one thing, I expected the kids to be here. And for another, that's not something I do. But…I am a big believer in making the most of unexpected opportunities."

He stilled. Then bristled. "So, what? You're offering me a pity—"

"I would never do that. Mainly because, for one thing, I don't pity you." She smirked. "Big difference between not being able to get any and choosing not to." Then she sobered. "I also know you're not ready to move on. That—emotionally at least—you might never be ready. And I accept that. But…" Her cheeks turning pink again, she nodded toward the tree, even as her lips curved. "But since I didn't get you anything for under the tree…" Her shoulders bumped.

He stared at her for a long, long time, then said, "I thought I was the one who owed you."

She finally unwound the scarf, only to slowly lift it over his head and around his neck, tugging him closer. But not too close. "Then this is what I'd call a win-win situation, don't you think? Giving, receiving… It's all good, right?"

He barely heard her gasp as his mouth crashed down on hers, as he released himself to the beast that'd been gnawing at his gut for weeks. He felt her hands tighten around the scarf, pulling him closer as her lips parted, and every scrap of control he'd clung to so fiercely fled screaming into the night. Dropping onto the couch before his bum knee gave out, he pulled her onto his lap, and she laughed, deep in her throat, as she straddled him, then kissed him again, a fearless, hungry kiss that shot straight to his groin.

Deeper, where the demons lived.

The skin under her sweater was sleek, smooth, hot as his hands roamed. Hell, it was almost painful, how much he wanted her…and guilt flashed, paralyzing him. Her breathing already ragged, Claire cupped his face in her hands, then touched her forehead to his.

"Second thoughts?"

"I haven't… Since Merri…"

"I know," she whispered. "Which is why this is your call. I'm only along for the ride."

"That doesn't seem fair somehow."

She sat back, her hands lowering to his shoulders, humor sparkling in her eyes. "Judging from what's pressing against me right now? Something tells me I'm not gonna have any complaints. Hey," she said softly when he looked away. "I don't expect you to ask me to go steady when this is over. This is only about now. About two people enjoying each other. Being with each other. Maybe working out a little stress. And the best part? Nobody will know but us."

"And Barney."

"Yeah, well, unless he's suddenly learned people-speak, I'm not worried."

"Except…dammit, Claire—we work together—"

"And I repeat—this goes no further than right here. Right now. I swear. I do not kiss—or anything else—and tell. We do this, we go on with our lives exactly as before. So. What's it gonna be?" Then she sucked in a breath, as though suddenly realizing something. "Oh. Wait. If you have issues with, um, me in your bed…"

Where you used to have sex with your wife, was the rest of that sentence, he guessed.

Ethan lifted a shaking hand and finally, finally sifted his fingers through those satiny, springy curls. "I bought a new bed six months…after. Couldn't sleep worth crap in the old one. But I'm not exactly…prepared."

"Didn't figure you would be. Lucky for you, I'm on the Pill. So we're good."

Speak for yourself, he wanted to say. "You're really sure about this?"

"You want me to smack you or what? And I do not mean as foreplay."

Even though fear still coiled inside him, he laughed.

And slipped that hellacious vest off her shoulders.

"Good choice," she said, smiling, and bent to kiss him again.

The first time was pretty much what you'd expect between two people who'd gone without for a while—hot, fast, a little awkward. Clumsy, even. And Claire had fully expected not only the clumsiness but that, once…relieved, Ethan would roll out of bed, either mortified or trying to act all cool, and suggest they order in Chinese or pizza or something. Or politely thank her, with a broad hint that she could go home now.

Not so, she thought as they lay all entwined and sticky and panting in his bed, and he whispered against her temple, "Was that as bad for you as it was for me?"

She laughed. "No, *bad* is when there's no fireworks at all."

"As opposed to their going off prematurely?"

"Hey. At least they went off."

He hesitated. "For you, too?"

She twisted to face him. "You seriously couldn't tell?"

"I was a little…preoccupied."

"Not to mention deaf. Jeez." When he didn't say anything, she hiked herself up on her elbow. "Please don't tell me you thought I faked it."

"Hey. You're the actress."

"And this isn't a damn stage. I don't pretend in real life."

One arm behind his head, he looked up at her. "So if you don't pretend," he murmured, lifting his other hand to lift her curls off her neck, which made her shiver and her nipples respond accordingly, "what's this all about?"

Something close to pain shot through her, that despite what she'd just said she couldn't answer as honestly as she would have if the situation were different. But the man was conflicted enough without her telling him she hadn't gotten naked with him simply because they were both needy and the timing seemed serendipitous, or that she'd never had sex with someone she didn't love, and that this time was no exception.

"It's about…friendship, I suppose. Caring. Giving," she said with a shrug. Then, trickling her fingers across his jaw, she grinned. "Having a little grown-up fun."

"You're really that much of a free spirit?"

Somehow, she kept the smile in place. "I really am."

"A free spirit who's been celibate for how long?"

"There's freedom in celibacy, too, you know. I'm not a slave to my body. Or its whinings. And you sure think a lot for a dude."

He almost smiled. "It passes the time while I work up to round two."

"Oh?"

Chuckling, he handily flipped her on her back so their fun bits could get reacquainted, and his weight was so welcome and warm and good she nearly passed out. "You didn't seriously think I was going to let you out of here with that initial travesty imprinted on your brain, do you?"

"So…you're saying you can do better?"

"Hey. Reputation to uphold here," he said, and dipped his head to demonstrate. Or, more accurately, begin to demonstrate. Because this time, no one was in any hurry. This time was about control and patience and sweet, sweet buildup…of exploration and experimentation and getting *really* intimately acquainted, of whiskers rasping against sensitive skin, a talented mouth sending sparks of startled

pleasure swirling deep, deep inside her...of a blissful pulsing that seemed to go on forever.

Then he was inside her from behind, in some clever position that apparently took pressure off his knee, his breath
hot on the back of her neck as he filled her, stroked her,
and, oh, my *word,* was he good at this...and then she was
floating, flying, crying out a second time—or third, if one
were being technical—over Ethan's own guttural release.

Then silence, save for their breathing, the incongruous
sound of Barney licking himself on the other side of the
room. Moonlight splashed across them, cold and unforgiv-
ing, such a contrast to Ethan's solidity against her back, his
hand warm and tender on her breast as he teased her nipple.

"Ho, ho, ho?" he said, and she laughed, even as the re-
crimination came so hard and fast Claire nearly lost her
breath. Because for all her knowing, *accepting,* that this
was only for now—and that her gift had been without
conditions—at that moment her intellect and her heart
were on opposite teams.

Then he gently rolled her over to gather her in his arms,
and she thought, *Not making this any better, bub.*

Another long stretch of silence followed, punctuated by
the steady beating of his heart against her ear, his fingers
rhythmically stroking her bare shoulder. Then, at last, a
long, shuddering breath. Claire shifted to prop her hand
on his chest and whisper, "How're you doing? And yes, I
want an honest answer."

"I'm not sure. This all feels a little...surreal."

"Bad surreal or good surreal?"

His chest rumbled. "Definitely not bad. But..." A small
smile on his lips, he angled his head to look into her eyes.
"How honest are we talking?"

"For heaven's sake, Ethan—I'm not some delicate little
flower." *Anymore.* "Just spit it out, already."

His brows drawn, he slowly swept her hair off her shoulder. "Merri was my first and only. Obviously. So I guess I'd always assumed that...doing this with anyone else would feel...weird. Like I was cheating on her." He gave his head a slight shake. "But it didn't. At all. Which is why it felt so surreal. Hell," he said on another breath, stuffing his hand behind his head again as he looked up at the ceiling. "I didn't even think about her. Not once."

"And now you're feeling guilty about that."

He blew a soft laugh through his nose. "A little. Yeah." His gaze shifted to hers again. "Sounds pretty messed up, huh—?"

On the nightstand next to him, Ethan's phone rang. Muttering a curse word, he fumbled for it, frowning at it in the dark before putting it to his ear.

"What's up?" he said, concern in his voice, as Claire took advantage of the distraction to haul herself to a sitting position, gathering the rumpled covers to her chin. "No, of course not....Carmela. Stop. Of course you can bring the kids home, I'm sorry John's not feeling well.... At least you guys got to see the show and the tree, right? Yeah, yeah....I'll see you all soon."

He cut off the call, then sighed. "It's my father-in-law. Guess he caught the girls' cold. Carmela says he was fine when they left, but it came on right as they got out of the show." He looked so apologetic Claire ached for him. "They'll be home in an hour. Um...you want to stay for dinner?"

"And wouldn't that be awkward?" Claire said as lightly as she could manage. "Although if you don't mind I think I'll take a quick shower before I go."

"Uh...sure. Here," he said, getting out of bed and walking naked to his closet to pull out a robe, which he handed to her.

"Thanks," she muttered, suddenly self-conscious as she wriggled into it before leaving the warm bed, saturated with the scent of their lovemaking, of Ethan, of her perfume.

"I'm sorry," he said as she pulled the robe closed, and she laughed. Sort of.

"For what? Having kids? Being who you are? And anyway," she said before he could respond, "it's not as if we'd planned this or anything." She tried another laugh. "I'm only glad I didn't get here any later."

"So...you're okay?"

"And you can stop with the foolish talk right now.... What are you doing?"

"Remembering," he said, sliding the robe open to pull her close again, hard against his nakedness as he joined their mouths in one last, heated, crazy-making kiss before letting her go, his expression every bit as tortured as she would have expected. Because now that reality—his reality, in any case—had once more reared its head... Oh, man. She could only imagine what was going through his head.

Claire lowered her eyes, grateful for the dark. That he couldn't see her tears, mostly in frustration with herself, for her own stupidity. For thinking she could do this without repercussions. Her words to Juliette echoed in her head...only Claire had done a lot more than let a boy kiss her in the janitor's closet.

So much for owning her decision, for feeling like an adult as well as acting like one. Especially when she realized Ethan was stripping the bed—still naked, heaven help her—dumping the pillows onto the floor, yanking off the sheets. Not that she didn't understand the prudence behind his action, but neither did she miss the symbolism that what they'd just done? Never happened.

"Use whatever you want in the bathroom," he said. "And there's clean towels in the linen closet."

"Got it, thanks."

A few minutes later, she was showercd and dressed, as purged of any evidence of their lovemaking as his bed, her hair a mass of tiny wet snakes around her face when Ethan—now dressed—caught her in the hall.

"You shouldn't go out like that, you'll catch cold," he said, his expression so conflicted Claire almost flinched.

"Old wives' tale," she said with a tight smile, one hand already on the doorknob. The dog at his heels, Ethan slowly closed the space between them to cup her cheek in his warm palm, kiss her mouth, her forehead.

"Drive safe," he said, and she nodded, then finally made her escape, coming as close to the walk of shame as she ever had. Or ever wanted to. Although at least she could get her own damn Chinese food, if she so desired.

Because autonomy was a beautiful thing.

Wally soundly scolded her when she opened her door, in all likelihood because there was a quarter-size bare spot in the bottom of his food dish.

"Yeah, yeah, you're in no danger of starving," Claire said, hefting the burgeoning plastic bag onto the two-seater bistro table wedged in her kitchen corner. Catching a whiff of the rich ginger-and-garlic aroma emanating from the bag, the cat immediately jumped up on one of the chairs, wiggling his pink nose.

"Git," Claire said, lightly swatting the beast off the chair, then sighed. She'd forgotten how hungry she got after sex, a thought that made her feel as if she'd been impaled by a chopstick.

As did the thought of eating alone. And no, the cat did not count.

Virgil answered on the first ring. "What's up, sweet thing?"

"You eat yet?"

"Oh, honey, ages ago. As befits a gentleman of my advanced years."

"Oh. Too bad. Because I kinda went nuts at China Garden."

"Oh?" A pause. Then, "Any spring rolls?"

"Six."

"I'll be right up."

She'd no sooner set her iPhone to play Christmas music—because she was nothing if not masochistic—than her bell rang, and there was Virgil, dapper as always in an argyle sweater vest and bow tie...and his house shoes. "My goodness, it smells heavenly in here," he said, then stopped with his hand on his heart when he saw her puny tree. "And isn't that the most precious thing?"

"There's one word for it," Claire muttered, arranging the open foam containers on her counter. "The spring rolls are in that bag, help yourself—"

"Oh, honey...what's wrong?"

Claire's eyes shot to his. "Why do you—?"

"Because I've seen that look on too many faces far too many times not to recognize a broken heart when I see it. And I'd love a cup of tea with this," he said, plucking one of the rolls out of the bag, "if you have it."

She grabbed the box of tea bags from the cabinet. "Then you need to have your eyes checked."

"That may well be. But my ears are fine. And you're a terrible liar."

A cup of water clunked into the microwave, Claire turned, her arms crossed. "Nobody broke my heart, Virgil." When he lowered his chin again, chewing, she sighed. "Fine, so maybe I got myself into something I shouldn't have, but I knew going in that..."

"That what?"

The microwave beeped. She retrieved the steaming cup, plopped a tea bag into it. "Okay, here's the thing... After my father died, it killed me, watching my mother grieve. Sure, I was sad, too, but she was…lost. So I decided I'd never let myself be that emotionally vulnerable."

Now seated at the table, the purring cat in his lap, Virgil rolled his eyes. "Well, hell. No wonder your marriage failed."

"Tell me something I don't know."

"So why did you get married in the first place?"

"Because that's what twenty-six-year-old women do? And I did love my ex—"

"But with half your heart."

"Ouch. But…yeah."

"You do realize how stupid that is. Not to mention impossible."

"Now? Sure."

"Which I assume brings us to tonight."

Claire yanked a pair of paper plates from another cabinet, silverware from the drawer underneath, and began scooping out Szechuan beef, pork fried rice, lemon chicken. "I honestly thought I'd made myself impervious to that whole heart-on-sleeve thing. That I was immune to the…messiness."

"Again. Stupid."

Butt now in chair, Claire shoveled in a chunk of chicken. "Again, tell me about it. And it suuucks."

"Sweetie, being in love doesn't suck—"

"It does when the other person is still in mourning for his dead wife."

"Oh." Dumping the cat so he could fill his own plate, Virgil frowned. "That could present a problem." Claire stabbed a chopstick in his direction. Virgil dropped a piece of chicken on the floor, where the cat pounced on it before it could fly away, then glanced over. "Does he know how you feel?"

She snorted. "Like he doesn't have enough to worry about without dealing with...that."

"As in, being loved?" Virgil gently said, and the food in Claire's mouth jammed in her throat.

She took a swig from her water bottle, then said, "Remember what I said about my mother? That's where he is. *And* he's got kids."

"Kids?" His plate piled high, Virgil sat back down across from her. "How many are we talking?"

"Four," she said, and Virgil let out a low whistle. "One of whom is my student." Her eyes filled. "All of whom I...I love to bits. Or could, if I let myself. Words I never, *ever* thought I'd hear come out of my mouth. But damned if those little stinkers didn't breach every one of my defenses...." She shook her head again, hard. "And Ethan... He's a terrific dad. Stubborn, sometimes. And crazy overprotective. But kind, and funny—in his own way—and...and just—" she sucked in a shaky breath *"—g-good."*

"Oh, honey—"

"But the point is, they've made a new life for themselves. A nice, safe life. A life I do not fit into."

"And why would you assume that?"

For the first time, doubt of another kind wriggled into her consciousness, even as she said, "Because the children... They don't need any more upheaval. Even... even if Ethan were up for giving this a shot...what if it didn't work out? The littlest one, especially—she's only six...." Claire shook her head, her chest aching.

Virgil chewed for a moment, then said, "So tell me something—when you audition for a part, do you hold back, afraid of looking like an idiot?"

She almost laughed. "No, of course not."

"What about in class? Do you dumb down the material, afraid the kids won't get it otherwise?"

"Well, no, but—"

"Then let me get this straight—you've fallen for with a man with four children, children you've admitted you love, as well. But you're willing to potentially deprive those children of a mother, not to mention their grieving father of a second chance at happiness—uh-huh, let that sink in for a minute—because you're afraid of what *might* happen? That does not sound like the Claire Jacobs I know. Because that woman couldn't be that selfish if her life depended on it."

Claire's mouth fell open. "But I'm only thinking of them—"

"Really? Because it sounds more to me like you're trying to save your own posterior."

"Virgil!"

"Yes, I get that you want to avoid the pain you saw your mother go through. I also remember your telling me about your childhood, how insecure you were. Especially around boys. Trust me, sweet thing, you want to talk terrified?" He raised his hand, then dropped it again, sighing. "Try growing up gay in the South in the fifties. However, we're not talking about me, we're talking about you. And *you're* one of the most generous people I've ever known. And that's a lot of people, sweetie."

"But—"

"And something else occurs to me. This Ethan... Do you think he'd give up those years he had with his wife— the children they had together—in exchange for not hurting now?"

After a moment, Claire shook her head. "No."

Virgil sneaked another tidbit to Wally. "Then doesn't he have the right to know how you feel? So he at least has the option to act on that or not?"

Claire met the old man's gaze for a moment before looking away. Outside, sparkling snowflakes lazily drifted to the yard below, like thousands of tiny angels. Like magic.

"Yes," Virgil said, his voice as soft as the falling snow, "there's always a risk, when you love, that your heart will get broken. But the rewards? More than worth the pain."

She looked back to see tears in her landlord's eyes. Behind the tears, though, happiness glinted. As well as a deep-seated peace that comes from knowing you've done your best.

That you've given all of yourself. Not only what you think you can spare.

A fitting revelation, she realized, for a season that was all about giving.

Nearly knocking her plate to the floor, Claire lunged across the table to hug him. "Merry Christmas, Virgil," she said, and he grinned. Then he reared back, frowning slightly.

"Are you aware you're wearing only one earring?"

"What?" Her hand flew to one ear, then the other. And sure enough, one of the tiny diamond studs her father had given her when she'd graduated from middle school was missing.

And since she knew she'd had them both when she'd arrived at Ethan's, obviously that was where it had fallen out.

Damn.

"Dad?" Staring at the glowing Christmas tree in the otherwise dark living room, Ethan looked up at Juliette's voice. The other kids had been in bed for an hour already. Apparently Jules had not followed their example.

"Yeah, honey?"

She sank onto the sofa beside him, Claire's earring glittering in her open palm. "I was putting your sheets in the dryer and found this on the floor. And I know it's Claire's because she wears this pair all the time."

And if there was a bigger "oh, crap" moment on the face of the planet, Ethan didn't know what that could be. She must've lost it in his bed, and it'd gotten tangled up in the sheets when he'd yanked them off. Bad enough he'd barely been able to focus on the kids all evening for feeling like his head would explode. Because he couldn't deny he ached for Claire in a way he only had for one other woman…a woman whose memory, despite that momentary lapse, had returned to haunt him immediately afterward. But even if he had been able to disentangle himself from the past, there was the small issue of Claire's insistence that their getting cozy had been a one-off. So the last thing he needed right now was his way-too-smart daughter's scrutiny.

Yet he somehow smiled and said, "Must've come out when Claire was here earlier. To deliver the presents for you guys?"

"Then how'd it get into the laundry room?"

"I have no idea," Ethan said mildly. "She was playing with Barney a lot—" Hearing his name, the dog lifted then cocked his head. "Maybe it got caught in his fur and he carried it in there?" He opened his hand, and Jules dropped the twinkly little stud into his palm. "I bet she'll be looking for it, though."

"Yeah, probably."

Jules pushed herself off the sofa to kneel in front of the tree, shoving her wild, blessedly streakless hair behind her ear. "Part of me can't believe she got us stuff. Except then I think—she's like the most giving person ever, you know?"

The ache intensified. "She really is."

His daughter plopped cross-legged on the floor, pulling the present to her into her lap. "She tell you what it is?"

"Nope. Good thing, right?"

That got a smile, sweet in the lights' glow. "You invite her to PopPop's for Christmas Eve?"

"What? No. I mean, it never occurred to me, since it's only family—"

"She gave us gifts, Dad. I think that qualifies. And no,

I'm not still trying to fix you two up, I've accepted that's not in the cards. But…she *feels* like family. Doesn't she?"

"She does," Ethan said over the knot in his chest. "You want me to ask her if she'd like to come?"

"Please—"

Ethan's phone buzzed. Did u find my earring?

He angled the phone toward his daughter. "Guess who?"

"Good. *Ask her,*" she said, then got up to give Ethan a good-night buss on his cheek before calling the dog to follow her upstairs, leaving Ethan to frown at the screen.

He could simply text back yes, as well as the invitation, and be done with it. But one, between his big fingers and the tiny keyboard, he hated texting. And two, after what they'd shared, texting seemed so…wrong. Although she had texted *him*….

Oh, for pity's sake—

"Yeah, I've got it," he said quietly when she answered. "Actually, Jules found it. On the laundry room floor."

Silence. Then, Claire said, "Is that bad?"

"I blamed it on the dog, said it must've gotten hung up in his fur when you were petting him."

Her laugh arrowed right through him, stirring memories he knew weren't going anywhere, anytime too soon. "Oh, you're good."

"I've had a lot of practice," he said, and she laughed again.

"I take it you're alone?"

"In a manner of speaking. Kids are all in bed, I'm downstairs."

"Recovering from tales of their big adventure in the city?"

Ethan smiled. "Something like that, yeah."

"How's your father-in-law?"

"He'll live, it's only a cold. Carmela has it a lot worse than he does, having to deal with him. Anyway—speaking of the kids—Pop always does this big thing on Christmas Eve. Juliette thought maybe you'd like to come?"

A pause preceded, "*Juliette* thought."

"You brought the kids presents, so she's seeing you as part of the family." He paused. "I promised her I'd ask you."

"And...are you okay with this?"

Ethan dragged a hand down his face, then sighed. "The truth? I'm worried about building up expectations—"

"No, no...you're right, absolutely. So tell her...I already have plans."

"Do you?"

"Like you said, kids don't always need to know—"

"Not asking for them."

Another beat passed before she said, "Not to go all cheesy on you or anything, but tonight... It was pretty damn special. For me, anyway. And this coming from a chick who'd pretty much given up on sex ever feeling special again. So why don't we simply leave it at that and call it good?"

It made perfect sense, what she was saying. Not to mention she was giving him the out that every man dreamed of. No commitment, no expectations, just a single, mind-blowing encounter that had made Ethan remember what it was like to have a life outside of his kids and work.

He should feel relieved. Free. Off the hook.

Instead, he said, "Sure. But FYI? It was pretty damn special for me, too," before he pushed End on his phone, fighting the urge to send the thing flying across the room.

"You chickened out," Virgil said behind Claire, startling the bejeebers out of her. She'd forgotten he was still there, cleaning up while she sent what was supposed to have been a straightforward text.

Clutching the phone to her stuttering heart, she turned

to her landlord. "You didn't hear the other side of the conversation, sweetie—"

"Didn't need to." A bag of leftovers clutched in one hand, he shook his head, his already thin mouth pulled so tight his lips were all but gone. "Honestly, honey—"

"Please don't give me some mishegoss about fighting for my man, Virgil—"

"Wasn't going to. Because until you realize *you're* the one worth winning, what the hell good would it do?"

Then he was gone, leaving Claire alone with a fridge full of Chinese takeout, a snoring cat and a hole in her ear where her earring should have been.

Not to mention one in her heart the size of Bayonne.

"But at least I've got my pride. Right, Wally?"

Cat didn't even bother to open an eye.

Chapter Twelve

Juliette understood how much her grandfather's Christmas Eve party meant to him, she really did. But while the grown-ups stuffed their faces and yakked with each other, and the little kids were all hyped up about Santa coming, she was seriously bored to tears. She also missed Scott, who was out of town with *his* grandparents and wouldn't be back until two days before New Year's. No, they still couldn't officially "date," but they were allowed to hang out at each other's houses—with close parental supervision, sigh—and you know what? For now, she was good with that. It was nice, actually, getting to know him as a person—a friend—without feeling pressured to do stuff she honestly wasn't ready to do, anyway.

But she really, really missed him.

Since she didn't feel part of the festivities anyway, she decided to go sit in the sunroom, in the dark, and enjoy a good mope. Only she nearly jumped out of her skin to find PopPop already there, sitting in the biggest rocker.

"Oh! Sorry! Didn't know you were in here—"

"No, no… Come on in, keep an old man company." Afraid to disobey—her grandfather could be a little scary, truth be told—she did, sitting on one of the wicker chairs close by. She sensed him watching her for a second before asking, "How come you're not with the others?"

Juliette shrugged. "Dunno. It felt weird, I guess."

"Weird, how?"

"Like…I didn't fit, or something. I guess because I'm the only teenager. What about you? After all, it's your party."

Pop chuckled. "Oh, it hasn't been my party for years. Not since… Well. Jeannie. But I still hold it every year. Because God forbid people think I've become a bitter old man."

"Are you?" Juliette asked, and her grandfather chuckled.

"At times? You bet. Mostly, though, I'm good. Even on those days when I miss your grandmother so much I can barely think straight. Like on the holidays. Gets really bad then."

"That's what it must be like for Dad," Juliette said, more to herself than her grandfather. "Not being able to think straight because he still misses Mom so much."

She heard her grandfather's chair creak as he shifted position. "In what way?"

"I…shouldn't… Never mind, I shouldn't've said anything."

"Which means you have to. And that's an order, young lady."

She smiled. PopPop could be gruff, but other than her dad there was no one she trusted more. "Okay," she said on a sigh. "Months ago I had this idea about getting Dad and Miss Jacobs together, which you probably already figured out."

"I did. Go on."

"Anyway…they basically both told me to mind my own business. Which was totally their right to do, don't get me wrong. And I really did back off, I swear. But all this stuff kept happening that sort of threw them together, and… Okay, I'm hardly like some old wise woman or anything, but now I think maybe they totally have a thing for each other, only neither of them wants to admit it."

"You don't say."

"Yeah. So now everything feels…wrong. Worse than before, even. And I know this isn't my problem to solve. That maybe it's not even solvable. But it still makes me sad. And being sad on Christmas Eve—"

"There you are," Dad said from the sunroom doorway, holding baby Jonny, and Juliette blushed—oh, God, had he overheard them? But all he said was "The others want to go caroling in the neighborhood. You in?"

"Are you joking? We never did that before."

"Yeah, well, your two new aunts can apparently get up to all kinds of mischief when they're together. And the consensus is, since you're the only one who can actually sing, they can't do this without you. So whaddya say?"

Juliette's first reaction was "no way." But then she thought maybe it'd be good, going singing in the crisp, cold night, oohing and aahing over everyone else's decorations. To at least try to get back a little of the magic she so desperately missed.

"Sure," she said, getting to her feet. "Sounds fun. You coming, too, Dad?"

"Nope, I'm gonna hang with Jonny. So you go on." He touched her hair. "Have a good time," he said, his smile not even beginning to mask the sadness in his voice.

And, as everyone got on their coats and hats and mittens, laughing and chattering, she silently prayed that her dad might feel a little of that magic, too. In whatever

way God—or whoever/whatever was steering this ship—
thought was best, since Juliette had no clue how to make
that happen.

"No, sit," Pop said before Ethan could make his escape.
"And give me the little squirt."

"He's nearly asleep."

"Then I won't wake him."

Slowly, Ethan put Jonny in his father's arms, where the
infant grinned, cooed and promptly passed out. "I only got
to hold one of my own like this," the Colonel said, adjusting the baby so they were both comfortable. "Abby. Rest
of you were all older when you came to us. So I can't get
enough of the grandbabies." He paused, then said, still
looking at the infant, "The holidays are hell, aren't they?"

After a moment, Ethan nodded. "Yeah. Pretty much."

"You ever think about getting married again?"

Ethan's laugh was dry. "No lead-in, just *bam,* hit a guy
between the eyes?"

"I'm too damn old to waste time on lead-ins. So?"

Despite his druthers, images of Claire flitted through,
of her laughing, decorating the tree with his kids…falling
apart in his arms… "No."

"Why not?"

Ethan blew out a breath. "Where would you like me to
start? Because, for one thing, it's taken this long for life
to finally feel normal again, especially for the kids. But
besides that…" He pressed his lips together. "I can't simply replace Merri. She was too much a part of my life—a
part of *me*—for too long. I mean, you get what I'm saying,
right? After all, you never remarried, either."

That got a piercing look the likes of which Ethan hadn't
seen since he was a teenager. "You know, I'm not gonna
deny that, twenty years ago, when you announced you'd
decided to go into the marines instead of taking that foot-

ball scholarship, I was so proud of you I could pop. Wasn't until later that I realized you'd done it for the wrong reasons. To please me instead of being true to yourself."

Wondering where his father was going with this, Ethan frowned. "That's not true—"

"The hell it isn't. Because I saw on your face, when you came home hurt and it was obvious you couldn't play anymore, that your dreams were as shattered as your knee, what you'd sacrificed. For what? *My* approval? My blessing? Your mother had said as much to me after you'd enlisted, but I didn't believe her. Didn't want to. Then Merri got pregnant, and you married her, and I know you loved her and all, but for God's sake, you were twenty-two. But you did what you thought you had to do. What you've always done, which is to put everybody else's needs ahead of your own."

"And how is that a bad thing? You and Mom always taught us to be unselfish, to do what was right—"

"That never meant leaving yourselves completely out of the equation. Because the longer you do that, the more you run the risk of not only becoming one miserable SOB, but of being not a whole helluva lot of good to all those people you're sacrificing yourself *for*. And yes, I know exactly what I'm talking about."

Jonny squirmed in his sleep, his face screwing up as if he was about to cry. But he settled back down, his breathing deep and even. The Colonel watched the baby for a moment, then said, "I felt exactly like you, after your mother died. I was convinced I'd had my shot, that the best I could do was adjust to my new life. And Abby was only fifteen— same age as Julie is now. No way was I going to shake things up any worse than they already were. Except…"

He looked at Ethan. "About a year later, this gal contacts me. Totally out of the blue. Wife of an old buddy. Except she was a widow by then. Wonderful woman," he said, shaking his head. "We struck up a correspondence, which was fun for a while...until I realized something was developing I wasn't sure I could handle. Or wanted to. So I used Abby as an excuse, and we stopped the thing dead in its tracks."

Stunned, Ethan stared at his father. "I had no idea."

"No one did. And now you're the only one who does. But by the time I got over myself enough to consider giving it another go, Marie was involved with someone else. Got married less than a year later, in fact. Can't tell you how many times since then I beat myself over the head for letting that opportunity slip through my fingers. For being a damn fool, for being afraid of a *blessing*."

"But...Abby—"

"Marie would've been a blessing for her, too. Except I was too boneheaded—and, okay, scared—to see it. All I could think was, I couldn't go through that again. Couldn't risk the pain." His mouth flattened. "Sound familiar?"

Ethan's gaze tangled with his father's for a long moment before he grimaced. "Maybe."

"Now, I'm not telling you to go out and get married tomorrow. But I am saying you need to stop letting a bunch of lies and excuses cut you off from the possibility of something good happening. For you *and* the kids. Sure, you've done everything in your power to get things back on track for them, like any good parent would. That's all well and good as far as it goes...except the only one not back on track is *you*. Everybody can see it, especially your kids. And if you love them, which I know you do, your only duty to them is to figure out how to fix that. You hear me?"

"Yeah," Ethan breathed out after a long moment, his brain still reverberating from his father's words. "I hear."

The baby protectively cradled against the Colonel's chest, he leaned forward and whispered, "Then go *do* something about it. Because gals like Claire—that one's special, son. And she's not gonna wait around forever for you to get your head on straight."

"What makes you think—?" His father actually laughed, and Ethan pushed out another sigh. "Fine. But…" He pushed to his feet, his hand clamped around the back of his neck. "Who's to say she'd stick around even if…" His heart punched against his ribs. "Even if I asked her to? What if she wants more than the kids and I can provide?"

"I take it you mean her career."

"Yes."

"Gal could've gone back to New York after her mother died. But she didn't. So what does that tell you?"

Ethan felt his forehead knot. "I have no idea."

"Then find out, dammit. Don't leave the question dangling, for God's sake. *Settle* it."

He glared at his father for a long moment before leaving the sunroom, grabbing his jacket off the front hall rack and escaping to the porch, where the cold air soothed his hot face. In the distance, he heard singing—his crazy family, he supposed, inflicting their holiday cheer on the unsuspecting neighborhood whether it was wanted it or not.

On a sigh, he lowered himself onto the porch steps, roughly scratching his head before knotting his hands between his knees. Overhead, clouds bunched, blotting what few stars could still be seen in the glare of everybody's Christmas lights. The chill made him stuff his hands into his pockets, where he found Claire's earring, safe in a little plastic bag. Why he'd put it there he had no idea. Except… he did, didn't he? To have something of hers—something of her—to hold on to, to touch whenever he wanted to. Until she reclaimed it, of course.

Now he pulled it out, watching it twinkle in the light from the twin coach lamps behind him, like one of those stars. Like that angel—Clarence, wasn't it?—in the opening of *It's a Wonderful Life,* a tiny star in the vast galaxy of forever...but with a crucially important role to play—to show a man that there was far more to life than only what appeared on the surface.

That you don't have to settle. Or ever give up.

On a shuddering sigh, Ethan lifted the plastic bag to his mouth, his eyes burning as he pressed the small diamond into his lip. Because Claire was his angel, wasn't she? His, and the children's, restoring to all of them so, so much that Ethan had believed they'd never have again. Hell, he'd never been afraid of risk before—not as a football player, or a marine, or when he took on a family when most guys his age would have run so fast in the other direction they would've burned up the pavement. So this loony tunes idea about wanting to keep everybody and everything in his orbit safe—including his sorry self, let's be totally honest, here—as though there really was some playbook for life, was not only unrealistic, it was flat-out stupid.

And, most important, it wasn't *him*.

Hauling in a huge breath, he pulled his phone from his pocket and scrolled through to Claire's number in his contacts, only to see the gang round the corner at the end of the block. A dozen voices, laughing and talking, drifted toward him on the cold night air, occasionally interrupted by happy, goofy woofing from Matt's and Tyler's dogs. Ethan pushed himself to his feet, slipping both phone and the earring back into his pocket, feeling the gentle assault of a light snow on his cheeks, his hair. As the group got closer, it began to split apart, Jules breaking away first to run to him. Even in the dark he could see her flushed cheeks and bright eyes, crumbs of snow dotting her curls as she grinned.

"Look who we found!"

Frowning, Ethan looked past her to see Claire in the midst of the pack, holding a bouncing Bella's hand, her other hand nestled in the crook of an older, shorter man's elbow. In front of them, the twins walked/skipped/stumbled backward, both yakking at the same time. She laughed at something Harry said.

Don't be an idiot, baby, he heard Merri whisper, clear as a bell.

And that was even before Claire's eyes met his, and she smiled, and damned if he wasn't George Bailey ready to lasso the damn moon for his Mary.

Not to mention toss that damned playbook right out the window.

At the expression on Ethan's face, Claire's heart started hammering hard enough to hurt. Then everyone else drifted inside the house—including Virgil, bless him—leaving Claire and Ethan alone in the snow, and before she could speak his mouth was on hers, warm and firm and shivery good, and it all felt like a damn Hallmark movie. Or at least one of their commercials.

And she thought, *Could be worse.*

A *lot* worse.

"You're not even going to ask me why I'm here?" she whispered when they finally broke apart, and he smiled.

"I know exactly why you're here," he said, brushing snow off her cheek. "Because you're supposed to be." Then he threaded his arms around her waist and pulled her as close as their winter duds would allow, and she thought, *Okay, I'm in.* "Although I am curious as to how that came about."

Smiling, she palmed the front of his jacket. "So I was putting together a puzzle with my landlord, Virgil. The short dude in the Santa hat? Anyway, we were in his living room when your entire fricking family shows up out front, singing their hearts out. So he drags me outside, and Juliette screams when she sees me, and then everybody was hugging and stuff and somehow we both got strong-armed into joining them. Not that Virgil needed much strong-arming," she said with a grin that immediately softened. "And it seemed like a good idea for me to go with. To, you know, make sure he was okay—"

"And that right there," Ethan said slowly, tugging her closer, "is why..." His breath warmed her face when he sighed. "Why we need you. Why *I* need you." He cupped her jaw, his hand warm, and she couldn't breathe. Or finish the sentence he'd interrupted. "Why I love you."

She blinked. "What?"

"I know. Totally nuts, right? Especially considering everything you've said, that you're probably not gonna stick around Maple River forever—"

"Oh. Ethan, I—"

"No, let me finish. Then you can do with it whatever you like. But..." He touched his forehead to hers. "But even if you tell me I've got the wrong end of the stick, that what happened the other night really was only for the moment..." He lifted his head to look deep into her eyes. "That moment... It unlocked something inside me I thought was closed up good and tight forever. Something I've been fighting like crazy for weeks." She saw his eyes get shiny, and her own vision blurred in response. "I didn't want to fall in love again. Didn't think I could. Or should. Then you came along and shot that idea all to hell," he said, and she choked out a laugh. "And for that, I will always love you. Even if you can't love me back."

"Oh, sweetie..." Half laughing, Claire braced her gloved hands on either side of that dear, dear face. "You certainly do have the wrong end of the stick. But it's not the end you think. Because you bet your sweet ass I love you back."

He actually flinched. "You...do?"

"Yes. Dammit. Because I didn't want this, either. Thought I didn't, anyway. It hurt so much when my father died. And watching my mother..." She sighed. "Then here you come along, and…" She sucked in an icy breath through her nose. "I was partly taking my cues from you, birdbrain."

"Oh?"

"Yeah, *oh*—whaddya think? And I'm here now because Virgil did everything short of tie a piece of tinsel garland around my neck and drag me here. But even if he hadn't," she said over Ethan's chuckle, "I already had my phone in my hand when your family showed up, ready to put my bodacious booty on the line. Because it finally dawned on me, in the midst of the most pitiful pity party in the history of pity parties, that my mother—God rest her sweet soul—would have clobbered me to the moon and back for being such a wuss. Criminy, what she and my father had was so sweet and wonderful and *fun*…. Why on earth would I want to deprive myself of that? Or at least…at least take a chance on it?"

Ethan's twinkling eyes searched hers for a moment before he said, very quietly, "And it occurs to *me* that this… half-life I've been living… That's not what Merri would have wanted for me. Or the kids—" He clenched his jaw, then whooshed out a breath. "Sorry, I—"

"Ethan. It's okay. What you obviously had with Merri… That's a huge part of what I love about you. And why…" She swallowed. "I feel so blessed. And honored. And the kids… Omigosh, I love them so much it hurts. I have no idea what to *do* with them, but I'm absolutely nuts about them."

"Yeah, well, *nuts* pretty much covers it," he said, and she laughed. "But…" His mouth pulled flat, he touched her temple so sweetly it brought tears to her eyes. Again. "The kids… They're kind of a 24/7 thing. You wanna talk about crowding your space…"

Her breath clouded around her face when she sighed. "And maybe it's about…the wrong people crowding my space. Because with the right people…" She reached to take her hands in his. "It's not crowded. It's…cozy."

At that, he laughed. Not a belly laugh, no, but a real, full-out laugh the likes of which she'd never heard out of the man's mouth until this very moment. And it was the most beautiful sound she'd ever heard in her life. "That's one word for it," he said, and she grinned. Then he sobered, "So…what're you saying?"

She swallowed past the tears. Of joy. Relief. "That I had no idea, when I came home, that I'd *find* home, too."

On a sigh, Ethan cradled her against his chest, kissing her wild hair. "But…all your plans?"

"To give Meryl Streep a run for her money?" Smiling, she reared back to look up at him. "Yes, performing's a big part of who I am, but it's not the whole of me. And there's plenty of local opportunity to do that, if I want to. But for now…" She took another breath and told her pounding heart to shut up already. "I think maybe…my time and energy would be better spent learning how to be a mom?"

Ethan cradled her face in his hands again. "And a wife?" he whispered, and her heart laughed and laughed and laughed.

"You really mean that?" she said, shaking.

"I've only ever used that word with one other woman," he said softly. "But only if that's what you really want. At least down the road—"

"Yes," she whispered. "I really do. I'd also really like you to kiss me again."

"Done," he said, and did. For a ridiculously long time. Then, holding up one finger, he pulled a little bag out of his pocket.

"Only diamond I happen to have on me. And it's yours, to boot, so I'm not sure how much it counts but…" He pinched the tiny stud out of the bag and held it up, where it twinkled madly in the porch lights. "They say when you leave something behind in someone's house, it means you want to come back. And I'm a big believer in signs."

"So...what you're saying is, if I take back *my own earring,* it means we're, like, going steady?"

Ethan grinned. "Works for me."

Claire giggled, then slowly shook her head. "Everybody will think we've lost our minds."

"Tough," he said, and tugged her close for another kiss, slipping the earring into the back pocket of her jeans as he did.

And then holding on tight.

Epilogue

Christmas morning

Dad grinned up at Jules a moment before she crashed beside him on the sofa, making him nearly spill his coffee.

"Sorry!"

Chuckling, he set it on the table beside him, then looped an arm around her shoulders as she snuggled up next to him, still in her jammies but smelling like the awesome perfume Claire'd given her, something she'd sampled—and totally loved—when they'd been shopping on Black Friday. From the stereo system, *The Messiah* blasted—the first time Dad had played it in more than three years.

Tugging Jules closer, he kissed the top of her head. "Happy?"

"You have no idea." She looked up at him, grinning so hard her cheeks hurt. Omigod—when her dad and Claire had come back inside at PopPop's last night and announced they were a couple, she thought she'd explode. The rest of the family was thrilled, too—well, duh—but especially her grandfather, who'd hugged them both harder than Juliette had ever seen him hug anybody. Juliette drew her bare feet up on the sofa, wrapping her arms around her knees. "And I'm not talking about the presents."

"Didn't think you were," Dad said with another squeeze, then laughed out loud when Barney bounced through the sea of torn wrapping paper after Claire's ginormous cat, whose hiss and smack on the dog's nose was total Jersey 'tude. Juliette laughed, too, even as her eyes stung... especially when Claire, sitting cross-legged on the floor with Bella's arms linked around her shoulders from behind and the poor dog in her lap, glanced over at Juliette with an understanding smile. Because Dad... He'd laughed more this morning than Juliette had heard him in the whole three and a half years since Mom died.

A thought that made Juliette stifle a giggle. Oh, Claire, who'd gone back to her place to get Wally, had started out the night in the extra bed in Juliette's room, and she'd been there in the morning, too. But when Juliette had awakened sometime in the middle of the night, the other bed had been empty. Didn't take a genius to figure out why. But hey, if it made Dad sound like that, more power to 'em, was all she had to say.

Wearing the new puppy slippers Claire had given her, Bella squatted to let the loudly rumbling cat—her new best bud—bump his head against her palm. Then the cat stalked to the other side of the room where the boys were up to their ears in Lego, rubbing up against first one, then the other, before plopping down between them with a smug kitty grin, his tail thumping against the carpet. As if he was happy to be home. And Claire... Well. Every time she looked up at Dad—which was only, like, every two seconds, she looked like she was pretty happy to be home, too.

In fact, everything seemed brighter somehow. Because,

Juliette realized as she unfolded herself from the sofa to go make the best Christmas breakfast ever, the glow was back.

The magic.

Except then she glanced across the breakfast bar to see Claire curled up on the sofa next to Dad, his arm around her shoulders and her hand on his knee, both of them with the most ridiculous, goony looks on their faces…and then the boys started yelling at each other and the dog got all up in the cat's face again, and she heard, over all of it, Claire's and Dad's laughter…and Juliette thought, as she hauled out the pancake mix, that this was a million times better than magic. Because this was *real*.

And she'd take that over magic any day.

* * * * *

MILLS & BOON®

Want to get more from Mills & Boon?

Here's what's available to you if you join the exclusive **Mills & Boon eBook Club** today:

✦ *Convenience – choose your books each month*
✦ *Exclusive – receive your books a month before anywhere else*
✦ *Flexibility – change your subscription at any time*
✦ *Variety – gain access to eBook-only series*
✦ *Value – subscriptions from just £1.99 a month*

So visit **www.millsandboon.co.uk/esubs** today to be a part of this exclusive eBook Club!